STOPPING FOR STRANGERS

Stopping
for Strangers

Daniel Griffin

ESPLANADE
Books
THE FICTION SERIES AT VÉHICULE PRESS

Published with the generous assistance of The Canada Council
for the Arts and the Canada Book Fund of the Department of
Canadian Heritage.

Esplanade Books editor: Andrew Steinmetz
Cover design: David Drummond
Set in Adobe Minion by Simon Garamond
Printed by Marquis Book Printing Inc.

LIBRARY AND ARCHIVES CANADA CATALOGUING IN PUBLICATION

Griffin, Daniel, 1971-
Stopping for strangers / Daniel Griffin.

Short stories.
ISBN 978-1-55065-320-5

I. Title.

PS8613.R5355S86 2011   C813'.6   C2011-905458-2

Published by Véhicule Press, Montréal, Québec, Canada
www.vehiculepress.com

Distribution in Canada by LitDistCo
orders@litdistco.ca

Distribution in the U.S. by Independent Publishers Group
www.ipgbook.com

Printed in Canada on FSC certified paper.

For my family

Kim, Evelyn, Tessa, Vivian

Contents

Thanks to my parents who have always believed in me and who have supported my writing from the very start. Thanks to Andrew Steinmetz, first for his persistence in bringing me to Véhicule, and then for his attentive eye, careful feedback and uplifting encouragement. Thanks to everyone else at Véhicule for going that extra mile in support of this book. I'm also indebted to all the teachers and students at University of British Columbia's Low Residency MFA. You were all wonderful to work with, and while I may have set a record by taking six years to finish an MFA, every day was worth it. Thanks to John, Ed, Harold, David, Gail, George, Sally, Ken, Tom, Paul, Andy, Zsuzsi, Tim, Cora, Matt, Britta, Pat, my widespread extended family, and everyone else who's had faith and supported my writing in various ways over the years. Influence and inspiration come in many forms. You've all given me more than you'll ever know. Thanks to my wife, Kim, my kids, Evelyn, Tessa and Vivian, always there for me, no matter what. Finally, thanks to our two cats, Tico and Patches. Neither a family nor a writer could ask for better companions.

"Mercedes Buyer's Guide" appeared in *The Dalhousie Review*, *The Journey Prize Stories 16* and *Coming Attractions 2008*, "Cabbage Leaves" in *The Antigonish Review*; "Stopping for Strangers" in *Grain*, "X", *Prairie Fire* and *Coming Attractions 2008*, "Promise", *The Wisconsin Review*, *Coming Attractions 2008*, "Florida" *The Antigonish Review*, "Lisa and Martin" *The New Quarterly*, "The Last Great Works of Alvin Cale," *The Dalhousie Review* and *The Journey Prize Stories 21*.

PROMISE

I slowed the car as we turned onto my brother's street. In the back, Tracy pointed her little hand out the window. "Is it that one?" she said. "Or that one, or that one?"

The houses were similar enough that I wasn't sure myself until I spotted the Gone Fishing sign. Marshall's drive was empty, the curtains were closed, and it was almost noon on a Saturday. It occurred to me briefly that he might actually be fishing.

Tracy had been asking questions about Uncle Marshall the whole way up, but now she didn't want to get out of the car. I had to carry her up the lane on my hip.

Marshall's Gone Fishing sign hung above a constellation of rust spots at the centre of his door. I reached out to touch it just as the door opened. My brother filled the space, rubbed his eyes then closed the door to remove the chain. "Well, well," he said. "Long time no see."

"Just dropping in for a quick visit." I tried to pull Tracy's arms from around my neck so she could say hello, but she tightened her grip and dug her face into the crook of my shoulder.

Marshall made space, and we followed him down the carpeted hall and into the living room where he collapsed into the corner of the sofa. "Make yourselves at home." Near his feet, the parts of a handgun were spread across a white towel—springs, levers, handle, barrel.

Mom had told me about the gun.

"Sorry to barge in, just—you know." I shrugged and filled my lungs. The disassembled pistol held my gaze. "Heard about Susan," I said at last.

"Figured that was why you were here."

"Mom's worried."

Marshall nodded a moment.

I crouched and faced Tracy. "Honey, you want to watch TV?"

"Susan took the TV," Marshall said. "And that makes her a fucking thief, but you probably don't want to hear that."

"We could get some toys, some books or a Barbie? Lets see what's in your backpack."

Tracy held it out and I unzipped it as I led her through to the dining room. My daughter has two sets of everything—one for her mother's place, one for mine. The toys in her backpack were from her mother's and less familiar to me.

"After we're going to the park, right?" she said.

"Absolutely."

Marshall's dining room table was littered with shopping bags, food wrappers and a few dirty plates. A small pile of unopened mail sat at one corner next to an empty bottle of Wild Turkey. When we were kids, Marshall and I had called the dining room "the dying room." As I crossed back through the kitchen, I said, "Looks like you're doing all your living in the dying room, Marshall." He didn't respond though. His expression didn't even change.

"She called me in hysterics," I said after a while.

"Who?"

"Mom. She mentioned a restraining order, assault charges. You getting a gun, which is obviously true."

"There's no assault charges, Doug."

"Okay," I said. "But—"

"—it's just Dad's Luger. Was getting rusty in Mom's basement so I'm cleaning it up."

"She's worried is all."

"So why didn't she come up and say this?"

My shoulders rose, a twitch of a shrug. I hadn't asked, but it had occurred to me that our mother might be a little afraid of Marshall. She might have also believed Marshall and I were closer than we were, that I might have access to some part of him denied to her.

I said none of this, and eventually Marshall said, "She'd rather have her errand boy do it."

Low in my guts, something turned over. "She probably thinks I can talk to you in a way she can't."

Marshall shifted in his seat and licked his lips. "And so what exactly are you supposed to be talking about?"

"I'm supposed to make sure you're okay, I guess. That you'll get through this. I mean—"

"—So tell her."

"Okay," I said. "I'll tell her." The words trailed away, and the room seemed suddenly cavernous, the space between us vast. Outside a robin swooped past and landed on the grass.

After high school, when Marshall and I began to veer apart, I'd started telling people that one of us had to have been adopted. Our trajectories continued to widen—he spent some time in the mili- tary, some time on probation, some time unemployed. I went to university, got a job, spent some time in the suburbs, some time at the Ministry of Transportation, some time in divorce court. These days we see each other for Christmas and most years that's it.

"Moment you came in, I figured you were here to kick me when I'm down," Marshall said.

"I get two weekends a month with Tracy, so I'm not about to waste—"

"—It's a power trip, Doug. That's all this is. Susan's fucking with me. Restraining orders are meaningless. I could get a restraining order against Mr Johansson for letting his dog shit on my lawn. Plus her mother made her get it." Marshall pursed his lips, scratched the tip of his nose. "We're working it out, actually. Couple therapy and stuff."

My head snapped up. "You're going to couple therapy?"

"Can't be any worse than talking to you."

"Okay."

"Doug, did you ever have a sense of humour?"

"And you can go to couple therapy despite the restraining order? Legally speaking, I mean."

"I was just over there last night."

"Over where?"

"Susan's mother's place. Where she's staying."

"What about the restraining order?"

He lurched towards me then—half launched himself off the sofa. I was a few feet away but still flinched. Marshall gave a shallow laugh, breathy and short. "You don't fucking listen is your problem."

I wanted to smile, but my face didn't cooperate. My right eye started twitching.

Tracy came trotting through the kitchen and into the living room. "Time's up," she said. "It's time to go to Old McDonalds."

"Okay, Honey, hold on a sec." I turned back to Marshall and took a deep breath. "We should probably go, but I'm glad you two are going to work it out. Mom will be happy to hear all this. I'm sure it's what she wanted."

Tracy gave my arm a pull. "Old McDonalds."

"Never met a woman who knew what she wanted," Marshall said.

I was ready to stand and go, but Marshall sat still. He was hunched in the corner of the sofa. Tracy pulled my sleeve again. "I thought we were going to the park," I said.

"Park, then Old McDonalds."

"Old Macdonald had a farm," Marshall sang. "Ee i ee i o."

Tracy turned towards him and a smile rose to her face. "That's not it. I'm talking about the Old McDonalds you eat at."

"That's just McDonalds. It's called McDonalds. Old Macdonald had a farm, Ronald McDonald had a hamburger."

"You're silly."

"Worse than silly. I'm stupid."

14

Tracy wrapped her fingers into the loose fabric of my sweater. She pulled herself close a moment. "Stupid's a bad word." Her voice was just above a whisper.

Marshall scratched at the stubble on his neck and leaned back. He didn't show any sign of having heard her.

"Listen, we should probably get going and leave you to it." I stood. "Next time you're down our way you should come by."

"There's a park down the road." Marshall gestured towards the street. "Swings and all that."

"Go get your things, Honey. I'll be right with you, okay?"

Marshall and I watched Tracy cross through the kitchen. "She's kind of duck-footed isn't she?"

Before I could respond, a siren wailed in the distance. We both cocked our heads towards the sound, and Tracy came running in. She pressed herself against me and covered her ears. Moments later the fire engine passed the house. The siren faded, then stopped all together. Tracy's shoulders dropped, but she kept her hands at her ears.

Marshall walked to the door. "Maybe the whole neighbourhood will burn, and I can get some insurance money."

While he leaned out for a look down the street, I took Tracy's hand. "Lets get your things picked up."

We collected her toys from the dining room. By the time we got back, Marshall was gone. I led Tracy outside. Billows of dark smoke rose from a house one block down. Two fire engines had their hoses trained on the fire, and Marshall was walking towards them with a stoop that hid his height.

Tracy raised her arms, and when I lifted her, she held on tight. Spilled water had pooled on the street and run down along the gutters, a little stream that had already reached Marshall's place.

I'd intended to simply say goodbye, but Tracy and I didn't reach Marshall until he was at the edge of a small crowd. He turned as we neared. "It's about time someone cleaned that place out. Fucking crack house. Whole area is going to shit."

A redheaded woman looked over. The heavy-set man next to her also turned. "You mind?" said the man.

"It's a crack house," said Marshall.

The man stepped closer and pushed my brother back. Marshall stumbled but recovered. Tracy screamed. Marshall raised his fists and took a couple of swings but a tall man grabbed him and held on. I instinctively backed away. I turned my body to keep Tracey's eyes from the tangle of people now gathered around Marshall.

"Just fuck off," the redheaded woman yelled.

I hurried back to the car, both arms tight around Tracy. "It's okay," I told her. "Everything's fine."

By the time Marshall caught up, I had Tracy buckled into the car seat.

"No park then, huh?" Marshall's shirt was torn open, but otherwise he looked unhurt.

"Call if you need anything."

"Doug, you are such a fucking shit."

"What?"

"I haven't seen you in what, six months, and you come up here and expect me to get on my knees or something."

"I'll tell Mom not to worry."

"You're just like her. You should have been born a woman."

I slid into the driver's seat.

"All our lives you managed to slip in and out, duck the worst of it while it lands on me. It really is amazing."

I started the engine, pulled out of the drive and waved without looking at him. Behind me, Tracy sniffled. She wiped her nose. At the first corner, she said, "Don't forget Old McDonald's."

"Will you quit bugging me about Old McDonalds?"

For a while after that, the only sound was the engine and the thumping of my heart. I adjusted the rearview mirror. Tracy was gazing out her window.

"Why were they fighting?" she asked

"I don't know, Honey. Uncle Marshall gets himself in trouble sometimes."

"Is he still in trouble?"

"I don't know. Hope not."

Near the highway, I pulled over for gas. While the cashier charged my credit card, I flipped through a phone book that lay on the counter. It listed Susan's mother's address on Helmken Street. I asked for directions. Back in the car, I told Tracy we had one more stop. "On the way to Old McDonald's," I added.

"Quick, okay?"

Helmken borders forest. Deep dark stands of cedar climb a gentle slope on one side of the street and tower over the bungalows opposite. Here people live on the cleaned-up corners of the land. Wilderness begins at the end of every street. Two steps off the paved road the world turns raw and wild.

I pulled over at number 218. "Sit tight," I said. "I'll be right back."

"Dad," she said, but I closed the door before she could say anymore.

The sun was high now and free of clouds. It warmed the crown of my head as I knocked. The door opened slowly, still chained. "Susan?" I said. "It's—"

"—He ask you to come?"

"I was just talking to him and, I mean. Are you two still seeing each other?" Susan leaned forward, she peered towards the car. The movement revealed the rest of her face. Purple feathered out from a dark ring under her right eye.

"Jesus," I said.

She watched me in silence.

"He talked about." I took a long, deep breath. "About maybe working things out, getting back together."

Susan shook her head and closed the door. Half of me expected her to unchain and fully open it, but instead the lock slid into place.

"I'll call the police if he sets foot anywhere near me. Tell him that."

〜

Tracy ate. I had no appetite. I drank coffee and watched while she ran around the PlayPlace.

One summer when Marshall and I were kids, we biked out to McDonalds almost every day. We took the money from our father's wallet. Eventually he caught Marshall with the wallet open. Dad caned him so badly that from where I was hiding in the attic, I could still hear Marshall scream. I was huddled under the rafters, head pressed hard against a wooden beam. A splinter cut into my cheek.

That was the summer Marshall and I formed a gang. It was just the two of us, but we had rules, daily meetings, we even had an oath of loyalty. The attic was our headquarters. It was up there that Marshall and I pricked our fingers and held them together, let the blood mingle.

When Tracy was done playing, I drove us back to Marshall's. The fire trucks were still in view, but the crowd had disappeared, and the smoke had thinned. Tracy leaned from her booster seat and held her face close up against the window, staring out at the trucks. "Wait here for one hot minute," I said.

Tracy didn't look at me. The fire trucks held her. "If my house burned down, I'd come and live with you," she said.

"That's right."

"Could Mom come too?"

"Of course."

I waited for her to say something more, but she didn't. She simply gazed out the window.

I knocked on Marshall's door until he answered. "You again," he said.

"Sorry about how things ended."

"Doug, you are such a pussy."

"After McDonald's we were about to head home, only I wanted to come by and say that. Mind if I use your washroom before we get back on the road?"

Marshall made space. I stepped inside.

"Keep an eye on Tracy for me? She's still in the car."

At the bathroom door, I turned and watched Marshall step onto the porch. Once he was out, I ducked into the living room and crouched before the disassembled pistol. I took the most important looking piece I could find. It was the hammer, the ignition system. It's wide and flat. Like an iceberg, the larger part hangs out of sight.

From the moment I left Marshall's house, I was expecting an angry phone call. I had images of him coming after me, but in the days that followed, Marshall never mentioned the hammer. He may not have even realized it was missing. As far as I know, he never tried to reassemble the Luger. And in the end it didn't matter. In the end, he used a knife.

THE LAST GREAT WORKS OF ALVIN CALE

I found out because of a dream. In this dream I was speaking to my son and asked how he was. "I'm skinny," he said. "Really skinny."

"How skinny?"

A long sandy silence followed. "Really, really skinny."

"Why?" I said, and he paused again, long enough it built a pressure inside me. Something awful waited.

"I've just become too skinny," he said at last.

That pulled me to a shallow wakefulness and I tossed and turned a while. When the clock said five, I got out of bed, made coffee on the propane stove and sat in the withering darkness. Although Alvin lives only a few hours south of me, we'd whittled our connection thin and I hadn't seen him in almost three years.

I should have made my way into town and phoned him right then, but once daylight held a steady grip on the land, I picked up my rucksack and a small canvas instead.

There's a cluster of giant firs I love on the flat land below the ridge—a cathedral that blots out the sky and encloses the forest floor. I set my stool in a well-worn spot in a bed of needles among the ferns and propped up the blank canvas. The painting consumed me as it always does, the physicality of the work, the concentration required to transfer life through my eyes and through the brush onto canvas. A day of work beat away the voices that dream had awoken. A week later though, I dreamed about Alvin again. He said he wished he wasn't so skinny. Pain and suffering lurked among those words. I was up early enough to watch the sun rise, but this time, once that ball of fire was clear of the trees, and its rays cut deep into my cabin, I walked out to the logging road, got in my truck and headed for town. The nearest phone's at the Shell station on the Pacific Rim Highway. I plugged in a quarter. Alvin's phone rang almost a dozen times. I was ready to hang up when Sally answered. "Hi," I said. "It's Skylar."

"Oh my God. Skylar."

The way she said that set off a depth charge within me. "Sorry if I woke you. If it's a bad time. Should I call you later?"

Silence. And then my son was on the line.

"I was wondering when you'd call."

I didn't recognize his voice at first. "Alvin?" I said. "What is it? What's going on?"

"Oh God, Dad. Oh Jesus. Didn't you get my letters?"

I live in a cabin in the bush year round with no electricity and no phone. It's Crown land and it was once a commune of sorts. This story truly starts there over thirty years ago. I was drawn to the West Coast by what Emily Carr had done, what Jack Shadbolt and Sybil Andrews were doing, and what I thought I could do. I was pulled into the bush by the dark rich colours of the earth, the filtered light and ancient trees. Alvin's mother and I built the cabin I live in now. At it's peak we were a community of a dozen souls—a draft dodger, his wife and their baby, a former math professor, a communist from the north of England, and a pair of sisters one of whom had adopted a son. Curious locals joined us off and on. And starting in the summer of 1974, a girl from Quebec named Sylvette Turcotte. I met her on a rainy day outside the Co-op. She had a striking face—deep set eyes, big and open. She'd travelled west with a boyfriend who now worked in a logging camp.

For almost three years Sylvette was my model. She was the source of the best work I've done in over forty years of painting.

She had an elastic body, graceful and elegant in every posture. She had skin that picked up dimples of sunlight, a figure that cast shadows upon itself. Even today I believe her body enabled me to see the human figure in a new way.

People in town called us hippies. They talked about free love. There was love, but it was never free. My wife left me a year after Sylvette arrived. Alvin stayed. He was sixteen by then and had begun to sketch Sylvette while she posed for me. Like Picasso, Alvin never drew as a child draws. He was proficient and precise from the day he began. Standing beside me in that cabin twenty some years ago, he captured her with simple strong lines, bold gestures with charcoal, pencil and eventually paint.

In 1977 Sylvette left and Alvin left with her. Sylvette was two months pregnant. She and Alvin lived together on Galliano Island and then on Salt Spring. This was the early eighties. I was lost in a short flash of fame built on those paintings of Sylvette. My only works in the National Gallery are of her.

Eventually Sylvette returned to Quebec. She still lives there, in Montreal. She has a daughter I've never met. The year Alvin found out about his cancer, the year I had those dreams and drove down island to be with him, this girl Lysanne had just turned twenty-five.

Alvin's wife Sally is short with a rolly-polly beauty—a plump frame, big cheeks. She met me at the door, opened it wide. "How are you doing?" I said

Sally backed off a step and raised the cigarette in her hand. "Started smoking again."

Alvin was on the sofa at the far end of their loft. The TV cast a trembling glow across his blanketed body. I wanted to walk straight over, but something held me a moment—a cocktail of anxieties: the possibility he was asleep, fear of what I was about to see, and the years of muck built between us, a weight like undigested meat in the belly.

Sally led the way and Alvin turned to face us. His nose was wounded, red and bloody looking. A gauze patch covered his right eye. The skin of his face, leathery and thin, looked ready to break apart.

I sent out a hand, but wasn't sure where to lay it. Eventually Alvin raised his own hand, embraced mine. "It's good to see you," I said.

He coughed, and it moved his whole body. He coughed again—took several attempts to get up the phlegm, and then he rested. He didn't speak, but he looked at me, one eye red-rimmed, worn and droopy. My own eyes filled with tears. I've lived a long life. I've stilled my heart more times than I can count, but here was my son, my only son, the child I raised. It took a moment to bring myself under control.

"Today was a radiation day," Sally said. "We just got back from the hospital. It's been a hard day for him."

Alvin turned his head, looked up at the ceiling. I glanced around the loft. Three walls were filled with paintings. It was all his work, but I only recognized one—a painting of Sylvette lying supine, face turned away. I knew it because he'd painted it standing beside me in my cabin twenty-some years ago. It had a raw fleshy power, a bold weight in colour and composition—amateurish, but strong and fresh. The day he began this painting is seared into me. On my own easel sat a brooding, shadowed portrait which I abandoned as though it were somehow tainted by the power of the painting emerging beside it.

Pablo Picasso's father, Jose Ruiz, was also an artist. He taught the young Picasso for years, but they had a falling out. The exact cause isn't recorded, but Picasso began signing his paintings using his mother's maiden name. Ruiz set down his brushes, gave painting up altogether in the shadow of his teenage son's brilliance.

Alvin noticed me looking over his paintings. He raised a hand. "Old work." It was a croak of a voice.

I took the rocker at the near end of the sofa. A newscast flickered across the TV, pictures of soldiers in desert fatigues. The volume was off. "The body's a miraculous thing," I said. "You'll see. Your body will amaze you."

"He needs distractions," Sally said. "Made me get him a TV. We keep the volume off sometimes so I can hear him." She handed me a mug of tea, sat at the far end of the sofa and lifted Alvin's feet onto her lap. "He listens to books on tape from the library. And we get a lot of movies."

After a time, Alvin began to snore, faint, raspy strokes. Sally patted his feet. "He's so glad you've come. We've been waiting, hoping you'd get his letters."

"I don't go into town much these days. Sometimes forget to check my mail."

In the early evening, Alvin awoke. He looked around. "I'm here," I said. "Right here." I took his hand in mine, dry and chapped, skin brittle from years of oil paints and turpentine, and after a silent moment, he closed his one eye and slept again.

He was like this as a boy—a fitful sleeper. He'd call out, his mother or I would come in, and he'd roll over and sleep again.

When Alvin next awoke, I lifted the paperback from the end table. It was a mystery by Tony Hillerman. On the cover was a human skull, a desert mesa in the background. "Shall I read?"

He held up a hand to stop me. A moment later he said, "I'm trapped in my mind. Not enough energy to do anything, but my mind still churns."

It was nine at night. He'd slept about six hours. "I drift through anxieties and worries, dwell on unsettled business. Probably all these drugs I'm taking."

I nodded and he raised his hand to his face, explored a moment.

"Remember how I wanted to live in town, wanted to go to school and have friends? I wanted so many things. A TV and a record player. A locker. Remember how much I wanted a locker?"

"Could have got you a locker if you'd just said."

"You and Mom were in la la land. She was stoned or drunk and you were painting or dilly dallying with someone or other."

"Oh for God's sakes, Alvin."

He turned his head to look up at the ceiling. "After you moved us up there, I mostly hated you. I thought I hated the painting too. Until Sylvette arrived. Although for a long time I just did it so I could see her naked."

"Why are you talking like this, Alvin?"

He shook his head and maybe he shrugged.

"You're going to pull through this—"

"—Dad," he said.

"Your doctor's good? I mean, you're happy with your treatment, your oncologist?"

"Sally thinks I should try something more natural. Diet based. Fighting fire with water not with fire."

"Sounds over-simplified."

"The work was flying out of me just a few months ago. I was exhausted, sleeping twelve hours a day, and painting the other twelve. Thought it was the work draining me. And then I started getting these headaches. For a month or two I assumed it was the turpentine. Tried different products, the fumeless stuff. Looking back there were six months of warning signs before I went to the doctor. That's what would have made the difference. Catching this six months earlier."

On one of the first days I was there, I came upon Sally in the kitchen staring out the window with her hands in the murky dishwater. I'd already done the dishes. It wasn't clear why she had her hands in the sink. She didn't turn around but seemed to sense my presence.

"I wanted a baby," she said at last. "I've left him three times because he didn't want kids. Each time he'd somehow pull me back, say he was ready. Never happened though."

She turned towards me, clasped her dripping hands. I took in a breath, but before I could speak, she said, "He can be a selfish bastard."

26

"Most artists are."

"So self-absorbed. He chose painting instead. Gunk covered canvases instead of a family, instead of a child to love."

"Some people aren't cut out to be parents."

"It's not that I don't love him, Skylar. But I'm forty-one, for God's sakes. I've spent ten years waiting."

"He's not much older than you, and he's fighting to live."

She shifted back a little, leaned against the counter. "See, I can't even explain it to you."

"He's my son."

"Forget it. Just." She turned and sank her hands back into the dishwater.

The woman who lived downstairs popped by that afternoon with her twin boys. They created a short-lived whirlwind of activity in the loft. While Alvin, Sally and the mother spoke, the twins chased each other and squealed. One rattled a toy car in circles on the hardwood. They started tossing paper airplanes about the room.

Later in the week there was a man with long matted hair which he pinned in a pile on top of his head. He didn't say much. He sat drinking tea with Alvin. Mostly, that's what I did too—sat beside him and drank tea. Sometimes I read to him, and when Alvin was up for it, we talked. One morning out of the blue he said, "I wrote to Sylvette. And to Lysanne."

The morning sun had thrown a great box of light into the loft revealing dancing particles of dust around us. "Do you think it's odd we never talked about this?" he said. "About Sylvette?"

"These things happen between men and women."

"Not that. I mean, not just that. I knew you used to send her money. Maybe because of that everyone involved was just as happy to let you think Lysanne's your daughter."

"Don't worry, Alvin. I put two and two together over the years." I didn't want to go down this road with him, didn't want a tour of the past. Maybe that's one of the attractions to painting. It's the very essence of living in the moment.

"And here I have a daughter I don't even know," he said.

"Alvin, I never claimed her. I never offered her my name. I simply sent some money. Truth is I've never seen her. There was plenty of time for you to take some responsibility."

Alvin was suddenly sweating, drops beaded on his narrow forehead. He wiped the sweat away and noticed me watching. He licked his lips, resettled his head. "I heard you and Sally the other night. Talking about kids and all. I guess I am a selfish bastard."

After a long silence, a fog horn sounded—a deep, lonely baritone. A still life that hung on the far wall caught my eye, a bright tapestry of flowers, vases and gourds. "Have you gone up to the studio?" he asked.

"Not yet."

"You know, this last creative spurt started with Sylvette. Painting the memory of her."

"Will she come visit?"

"Don't know."

"Who else did you write? Besides me, I mean."

"Mother."

"Alvin. How." I cut myself off. "She's been dead five years, Alvin."

"What am I saying? I mean." He looked like he was forcing himself to smile. "Oh God, I don't know what I mean. I'm just so tired I can't think straight."

"Rest," I said and leaned closer to pull up the blanket. "Just rest."

If he hadn't mentioned Sylvette, I might not have gone up to his studio. And without seeing those paintings before he died, I might have left them as they were and gone on painting in obscurity the rest of my life. But that's not how it happened.

In the morning, with the brightness of early sunlight, I pulled paintings from slots, removed drop cloths, set canvases around the room. They were paintings of pain and suffering—fire, bodies, war and destruction—figures melting into shapes and colours, wild brushstrokes on every canvas, a firm, ambitious movement. They were a horror story of a mind that seemed rawly touched by death. And I couldn't take my eyes away.

In most, the figures were unrecognizable, but there was a series of small portraits of distorted and blasted faces. Sylvette was a mere memory on the canvas, but I knew it was her.

For almost an hour I looked over the paintings, not as a critic, nor painter nor father. They connected beneath that, connected with the human through the primordial visual—the sense that travels directly to the soul and can make it shudder.

When I returned to the loft, the man with the dreadlocks piled on his head was sitting in the rocking chair. I lingered at a distance, waited until he was done his tea then walked him out. At the door, he said, "Think positive thoughts. Give him your positive energy. It's making a difference already."

When I returned, Alvin was asleep. I rocked by his side while images from those paintings coursed through my mind—the burning colours, the lopsided composition, the twisted faces, figures sprawled across canvases. When Alvin finally awoke, I took his hand. "They really are quite good," I said after a moment.

His one eye focused on me, bloodshot and red-rimmed, it was hard to return his gaze. "If it weren't for the fact they're in my studio, I wouldn't be sure they were mine."

"They're an achievement." This was another understatement, and I should have said more, but the generosity wasn't in me.

"Just before you called last week," he said. "I went up there. When I looked at them, even with just one eye, I could see that I was dying."

The next day, I drove back to Tofino, back to my cabin and the bush. I arrived at dusk and slept. In the morning I began to paint. The only cabin I use is one large room with windows facing every direction and a bedroom loft above the little kitchen. The rest of the space is studio—floor spackled with paint, two easels in the middle alongside a large white mobile wall. I use a narrow counter at one end of the room as a pallet. The other side of the room is racks and slots for paintings. Space is so tight I've removed most older canvases from their frames and rolled them.

That morning, I began from the bones of abstract work I'd done off and on the past two years—a dozen paintings that were not yet realized. My best work comes from painting over an existing piece, starting again without starting again.

For eight solid hours I worked with brush in hand. Painting's physical and draining, but I worked on three different canvases before I lay down and slept. Over the next five days all I did was paint, sleep and eat. I pushed until this old body teetered on the edge of collapse. And then I went into town. It was Monday, two days after Alvin's second to last radiation treatment. Someone should have been home, but I called all day without getting through. I left two messages and then checked at the post office for any general delivery mail. There was a card from Alvin postmarked in July. "I have stage 4 cancer. I'd like to see you. I'm writing because I don't know how else to get in touch. Will you come?" Some words were scratched out. At the bottom he signed it only with an A.

My body slumped against the post office wall. The card was two months old, and although I told myself that, I couldn't help but read it as today's news. The clerk stepped from behind the desk, but I waved her off and managed to stand.

I returned to the cabin to sleep that evening. The last quarter-mile along the ridge was a struggle. My legs were watery weak. Twice I had to rest where I wouldn't normally even pause.

I returned to town that Wednesday. Sally answered the phone. "They've stopped the radiation." That was the first thing she said. "They found more cancer. In his brain."

"I'll be right down. I'll come tonight."

"We're leaving this afternoon. There's an alternative treatment centre in Tijuana. We've been considering it for a while. Sort of famous for holistic treatments."

"And they say they can help?"

"They're willing to try."

"Sally, it's a long way for him—"

"—Let me put Alvin on. Hold on a second."

Alvin grunted into the phone.

"So she won that battle," I said, meaning it to be light-hearted although I knew it didn't sound that way.

"There's only one battle here, Dad, and we're all on the same side."

"I know. I'm sorry."

"So am I."

"If these are your last days, Alvin, don't spend them in Mexico. You could paint. We could paint together."

"I've lost one eye. I'm half blind in the other. I'm just trying to live, Dad."

"Do you want me to come with you?"

"I don't know."

My fingers ran down the pad of buttons on the phone, touching but not pushing. "I've been working since I saw those paintings of yours. They've travelled with me. They live in my mind. Best thing you've ever done."

"I know. Even when I was working on them I knew. It was like I'd channelled something, brush guided by a force beyond me. As though the paintings weren't even mine."

It took me an hour to walk the path back to my cabin. I had to rest at every chance. It took two days before I could pick up my brushes. Even then all I could do was stand and stare. All my life I've thought I had something to say. Pile all my paintings end to end and they couldn't whisper a word of comfort now. I set down the brushes, looked out the windows—out over the ocean, across the great expanse of grey which meets the sky in a fine thin line.

That weekend I bought a roll of quarters. At the library, I wrote down every number for a Sylvette or Lysanne Turcotte in Montreal. I called them all from the pay phone outside the Co-op with no luck. When I was done, I called Alvin's neighbour for an update.

"What am I supposed to know?" Sue said. "What am I supposed to tell you? They just left."

Back in my cabin, I set those abstracts in storage slots and worked in the garden. My marijuana crop was ready. I harvested it, carried it into town and from there called Sue again. She said they were giving him some tests. That was all. No other news. I spent the rest of the week putting frames together. I gessoed them, then drove back to Victoria.

Alvin and Sally kept a spare key under a flower pot. Up in his studio, I lay the paintings out, drank from them again then gathered together the half a dozen smallest canvases, the portraits I believed were of Sylvette—her face melting away into abstract forms. These I took with me.

In my studio the next morning, with those portraits of Sylvette arranged behind me, I raised my brush and stared again at a blank canvas, bent close until I could make out its dimpled skin, could smell the dried gesso. At the bench, where all God's colours are squeezed in drips and drabs, my brush dipped into the azure blue of a summer sky. Standing at the easel I turned slowly and faced Alvin's paintings. I crouched by the first—a rich vision of a face turned raw and bloody across the top of the painting. It was as though the skull had been sliced open and the top lifted off. The face itself was green, grey and blue and I brought my brush so close to the dark shadow of the nose that it might have touched. I backed away, dropped the brush and for a moment paced the room. I walked end to end, looked out at the ocean. Two container ships hung on its edge, grey shadows out there on the horizon.

At last, I returned to the painting. I raised my brush and this time it did touch.

In the early-1900s, Chaim Soutine used to send an assistant to buy paintings from hawkers on the banks of the Seine. He'd use these as a base. He'd begin from them. I'd done similar things, although never with a painting of my son's. In one way or another every artist works from the paintings of others. We all take and we all give. It's the cycle of art.

Next morning I returned to town and called Sue. "They're coming home," she said. "Going from the airport straight to the hospice."

My body went slack. I leaned against the phone booth to stay upright. My mind had formed a scale from worst news to best and this was as close to the worst as I'd allowed myself to consider. I managed a few words of thanks into the receiver, backed out of the booth and walked away.

The Sooke Hospice is a quiet retreat in the hills—a peaceful place where people go to die. I arrived in the evening after a rain. The earthy smell of a warm damp garden was rich in the air. A woman in a black leather coat stood smoking under the awning. At the reception desk a nurse greeted me and led me down a short hallway. Alvin was propped up in bed, ashen and gaunt—the withered branch of an ancient tree. Sally was curled in the chair beside him, and my entry woke her. She rubbed her eyes, and Alvin turned my way. He seemed to smile as he raised a hand. He said something, but it was just a croak.

"Lysanne," Sally said. "She arrived last night." And then the woman in the leather coat was at the doorway. Her stringy black hair fell over her face, but even through that veil she looked like her mother—the strong jaw and muscular face, shoulders set at attention. This could have been Sylvette walking into our lives twenty some years ago.

Sally stood. "Lysanne, Skylar."

Lysanne stepped forward. "How do you do?" She rose to her toes and kissed my cheek. "I do not speak English well." She flashed a wide, embarrassed grin, almost giggled.

I turned to Sally. "I didn't know. You should have told me."

Alvin raised his hand for Lysanne. He spoke little above a whisper, and she leaned close to listen. When she backed away, Alvin managed to sit up, and with our help, he stood. He posed for a photograph with me and Lysanne. We rang for the nurse. She took another, which included Sally, then one of just Alvin and Lysanne, one of him with Sally, and finally one with me—the two of us trying to smile, my arm around his bony shoulder.

Alvin slept and Lysanne went out to smoke again. Sally joined her. Alvin's rib cage barely registered each shallow breath—every one was a labour to produce. His face, once round and full, had been chiselled away. It was now just bone and skin.

Sally returned and I listened as she made herself comfortable. "So?" I said after a while.

"So," she said.

"Lysanne."

Sally nodded, gestured outside. "She's talking to someone on the phone."

"I didn't mean that. I meant—"

"—I know what you meant."

I stretched out my legs.

"He's happy," Sally said. "It's made him happy." She leaned her head back and for a moment she seemed to be waiting for sleep. "Months ago, when we first talked about going to Tijuana, it seemed so expensive. In the end, the money was nothing. It was the cost in time. It really just exhausted him. He could have spent a few more days with Lysanne. A few more days at home."

"I know."

"It feels like it's been so long, but really it's only been three months. Hardly a beat of time." She raised her head, opened her eyes and looked at me. "Sometimes I wonder if all this effort to prolong life was more for me than him."

"Have you talked to him about this?"

"In a way."

"Now's the time. I mean, if it's important, don't let him go without talking this through."

She snorted. "That's rich, you telling me I need to communicate. The things the two of you need to talk through could fill a book."

34

I did my best to smile, but I knew it wasn't coming through. "Maybe that's it. There's so much there's effectively nothing."

"That's one way to look at it."

"We connect through our work."

"That's a bullshit answer."

"What do you want from me, Sally?"

"I don't want anything from you. Maybe Alvin does though. Maybe you do, but can't see it."

"I believe it's possible to connect through art, that painting brings us together on a different level. I know you'll never understand, but it's true."

We sat with him through the night, the three of us, alternately holding his hand, brushing the sweat from his forehead and rubbing his bony feet. In the morning, he asked for more morphine. Sally climbed into bed with him, curled against him while the nurse increased the dose in his IV. That evening he died—a last rattling breath and then nothing. Stillness. Peace.

"Will you leave me with him?" Sally said. "For a while."

Lysanne led the way into the damp night, into the sweet, rich smell of autumn. The moon hung full, in the sky, heavy and white, ready to fall earthwards. We got in my truck and drove into town.

I switched on all the lights in the loft and took Lysanne to the sofa where Alvin had spent so many of his last days. This was the only painting of Sylvette left in the house as far as I knew. Lysanne gazed at it and nodded. "Sylvette," I said. "Alvin. He was little more than a child. So was your mother."

I went to prepare the bed for her and when I returned, she was sitting on the sofa, arms folded, alone in her thoughts. I sat and took her hand, squeezed it, this soft still hand of the only child of my only child.

From the moment I'd stepped into the loft, I could feel my son's paintings. They called to me, the last great works of Alvin Cale. Although I sat with my granddaughter, my mind was already heading upstairs, and although I told myself I wouldn't take them, I knew it was a lie. I knew before the next day passed all those canvases would be in my truck. This knowledge, wrapped tight in shame, ate away at me while my granddaughter wept.

CABBAGE LEAVES

The lights went out and the image on the TV shrank to a dot. "Fuck," Sam said. The dot disappeared. Sam twisted around and peered between the curtains. Across the street the houses were dark. His nose touched the glass and his breath fogged the window. "Power's out."

At the other end of the sofa, Liz yawned and sat up. "I'd better go feed Ashley." She edged forward on the sofa and drew both hands down her face as though to wipe away sleep. "Look at this. Look at my shirt. I'm starting to leak."

Sam didn't look though. The TV had his attention again. The screen gave off an eerie, grey glow as if it had found a couple of amps in some forgotten part of the grid. "I was right in the middle of this weird travel show." They'd been watching MuchMusic when Liz fell asleep. Afterwards Sam had flipped through channels, but the remote was acting up and had left him stranded on PBS. "It was about this town in Italy where people throw oranges at each other. It was kind of funny."

Sam waited for Liz to respond, but she didn't. She stood, arched her back and shoulders, stretched out her arms.

"Way back when the peasants rebelled against this king who used to spend a night with all the new brides. When you're king everyone does what you say, so after every wedding, brides used to hop up to the castle for the night. Until this one girl refused and set off a big rebellion. The peasants and whatnot didn't have any weapons so they threw rocks."

"Is that it? Is that the story?"

"The whole time they were showing this, I kept thinking that if we'd lived back then you wouldn't be so upset about not being married."

"I have to feed Ashley."

"Oh, come on, Babe. I'm joking. Relax a second."

Liz stubbed her toe on the way to the bedroom. She didn't say anything, just gasped and held her foot a moment. Sam shifted around, peered out into the night. Complete darkness. "What do you think would happen if the power never came back?"

"Would you get me a flashlight? Something so I can see?"

Sam felt his way through the livingroom, down the hall and into the kitchen. He switched on the gas stove, used its flickering light to go through the drawers.

Liz was leaning over the crib. Sam moved close. He aimed the flashlight at the wall so it spilt a faint light across Ashley. She was on her back, blankets tangled at her feet. Her face looked relaxed and she breathed so slowly it was hard to be sure she was breathing at all. Liz leaned in, brushed the back of her hand along Ashley's cheek. "We still haven't gotten her tetanus shot. Doctor Haas's secretary called work just to say that."

Sam nodded. He thought she'd had tetanus, but he might have been confusing it with rubella or one of the others, so he didn't say anything. He didn't want it to sound like he wasn't paying attention to his daughter's health.

"Can you imagine if she got tetanus this week, got it before we went for the shot? I mean, I don't know what the chances are. Not very high, right? It makes you think though."

"Lots of people don't get any of those shots. Plus you only get tetanus from rusty metal."

"Oh."

Sam raised the flashlight, shone it in Liz's face. "Now tell me," he said.

She turned away. "Tell you what?"

Sam didn't know what to say. He'd just been messing around. In the silence that followed, he lowered the flashlight. He considered suggesting they drink some beers or get out the bong, but he doubted Liz would go for it. Plus he was getting tired. Bed would be all right. He had to be at work at eight.

"You think I'd make a good king?"

"A king?" Liz turned to him. Moonlight touched her face.

"You'd be the queen which is almost as good. Everyone but me would have to do what you say."

Liz ran a hand along the smooth wood of the crib until she touched the mobile. The contact made it quiver. The farm animals above Ashley began to turn. "On the way home yesterday we were at this one stop a long time, and for some reason my mind pictured a baby sitting in the shelter and it just occurred to me, what if someone had left her baby there? You think that could happen, someone forgets her baby the way you forget groceries?"

"Someone would notice. Everyone looks out for babies."

"What if she was the only one at the stop?"

"You don't just forget your baby. That's what all the hormones are for. To develop attachments. It would be like forgetting your right arm."

Sam aimed the light at Liz again. She turned and reached into the crib, carried Ashley to the bed.

Ashley nursed for a minute then pulled away. Liz brushed Ashley's lips with a finger, blew on her face. The baby suckled again, but only briefly. "She's self-weaning. That's what she's doing. I read about self-weaning. She gets too much bottle." Liz tried once more but Ashley wouldn't even open her mouth. She set the baby on the mattress, rested a hand on her forehead.

"It's good that she's sleeping. She needs to sleep. We should do something. We should have some fun."

"Fun like maybe watching my boobs split open." Liz pulled down her shirt. "Jesus, this one's like a rock. All she did was get my milk started."

Sam shifted closer. "Come here. Come here and let me see."

"Sam," she said. "Sam, don't."

"What?"

"I'm not in the mood."

"I was only touching. I wasn't asking for anything."

"They're just tender." She pushed the extra pillow onto the floor, slid down on the bed. "Can you at least go get the book? Can you at least see what I'm supposed to do."

"Supposed to do?"

"About engorgement. Read about what to do so they don't burst."

Sam took the flashlight into the living room, flipped through the baby book. It said to use cabbage leaves. It suggested cold packs, hot packs, pumping or hand expressing. He shone the light towards the bedroom. "We have any cabbage leaves?" Liz didn't answer. He read two paragraphs to her then checked his watch. Almost ten. The grocers on Mason might still be open. He brought the book in, opened it to the page with diagrams about hand expressing. "I'll be back in a jiffy."

The store was getting ready to close. Both awnings were rolled in and a wiry man wearing a white apron was pushing one of the outdoor produce stands up a ramp and inside. Sam followed. The man pushed the stand past a bank of coolers to a spot in front of the candy bar display. Sam lifted a cabbage off the top shelf.

Only one register was open, and the line was long. Sam passed the cabbage from hand to hand and watched the girls in front of him. They were about Sam's age, maybe a little younger. Probably students, although they didn't dress like students. They looked ready for a night out. They wore little dresses, black and clingy. Not much to be wearing on a night like this. Sam leaned forward a bit. He tried to be discreet. The girl closest had bobbed hair cut high enough that it gave a grace to her long neck and her bare shoulders. She glanced back as she stepped towards the cash. Sam returned his eyes to the cabbage. It was a veiny, wrinkled old thing. There weren't many vegetables uglier than a cabbage.

When Sam looked up again, the girl had both hands held out for change. Her bracelets tinkled.

Halfway up Davenport, Sam heard a car honk. He turned. Someone was leaning out the passenger window. "Sammy. Sammy boy." It was Jeff Sorenson. Sam waved. The car rolled past. "Show us your snake, Sammy." Near the end of the block, the car slowed, stopped. Sam ran for two or three steps then the car lurched on, turned the corner and disappeared. It was Ollie's car, mufflerless with a broken tail light from when he'd backed into a Brinks truck.

They passed again when Sam was on the next block. Jeff was still leaning out the window. "Sammy Jenkins blows dead dogs." The car squealed as it took the corner. Sam paused at the curbside. He tried to think of something to shout. He tossed the cabbage from hand to hand. He could throw it at them next time they passed, try and get it through the open window. Picture the look on Jeff's face then.

At the end of the block, Sam turned up Hastings. He looked back a couple of times to see if Ollie and Jeff were approaching.

The apartment was lit. Sam couldn't make out any movement through the curtains. He climbed the stairs, searched for his keys. Eventually he raised a hand, but instead of knocking, he just lay it softly on the door, rested it there, fingertips on the smooth paint. Inside it would be warm, his daughter asleep, Liz waiting. He leaned close and touched his forehead to the wood. "Liz," he said. "Liz are you there?" He tapped lightly, fingers playing against the panel. His breath curled off the door and brushed his face. "Are you there?"

Sam was only whispering, but he thought somehow she would know. If she was truly waiting for him, she would hear.

Sam raised his voice a little. "Liz?" And then he heard her, moving towards him.

The Leap

The Ugly Duck was closed, so my brother Marv directed us up Dufferin, past St. Clair to a bar called Dixie's. It's in the back of a concrete bunker of a building. Above the door a red neon sign spells the name in bold looping cursive. We parked in the stall nearest the entrance, and I pulled out my brother's chair and waited in the drizzle while he shifted from the passenger seat.

Dixie's was almost empty: just a couple of men at the bar and a waitress cleaning glasses. Marv wheeled ahead with his pool cue in a box on his lap. He had to push a couple of stools aside to get through. As we passed the bar he gave a wave. "My sister and me came to shoot pool."

The bald man on the far stool raised his glass to us. At the back of the bar, I set quarters in stacks of four along the edge of the pool table. Marv assembled his Tiger X cue while the waitress approached, drumming fingers on her jeans. My brother ordered a shot of vodka plus a Blue. I ordered coffee. Marv wheeled back a little, turned one way then the other in a sort of wheel chair dance.

Before the accident, Marv was a gymnast. We both were. Pommel horse, parallel bars, mat work. As teenagers we did combined routines in acrobatic gymnastics—a brother-sister duo. We made nationals the fall I turned fourteen. The next year Marv started university and his old routines became party tricks—a balance beam act on the rail of a deck, flips across lawns. There was drinking involved the night it happened. He leaped off a porch, thought he'd land on his feet. That was six years ago. Everyone now refers to it as The Accident, but the way I see it, although it certainly wasn't deliberate, it wasn't entirely accidental either.

Pool balls tumbled down the chute and gathered at the end of the table. I racked them while Marv rolled past studying the field of play. Once the balls were huddled in a tight triangle, I chose a cue and perched myself on a stool.

We'd started these outings two years ago after I found Marv passed out on his bathroom floor. Off and on since the accident, Marv's lived in the bottle. On that particular night, I decided more routines would help. Give him an outlet, a passion. The next morning we talked, and he chose pool.

When the problem is drinking, it's odd to agree on regular outings to a bar, but I set rules around it. I wouldn't pick him up if he'd been drinking. I'd pay for the pool and for my coffee but not for alcohol. Only beer was another rule, although he often ordered a shot to get started. That was a compromise. Something I'm not normally good at.

Marv had a rule of his own: he wouldn't play without wet lips and that's why we were sitting there watching a set pool table. His way of suggesting that even on our Sunday outings pool came second to drinking.

I edged off my stool to see how the waitress was progressing. The bald man waved. "Want me to break them for you? Get you all started?"

Marv wheeled around. "Think a man in a chair and a short girl can't play pool?"

Bars like Dixie's draw a rare current of machismo from Marv. He's always been muscular, but his voice deepens, he squares his shoulders. There's a Budweiser tint to the world in here. That's probably part of the appeal.

The waitress stepped from behind the bar and strode over. She set down my coffee, Marv's beer and his vodka then gave Marv a snapshot smile. "I figure anyone who brings his own pool cue must know what he's doing."

The balls scattered. The seven went down. The others found places spread across the felt. Marv wheeled around the table and lined up shots that looked like they were waiting for him, like they were specially prepared. His chair put him at the perfect height for pool: eye level with the balls, no need to bend or crouch. By the time I was up, the solids were all but extinct.

We'd played pool just about every Sunday for two years, and although I was still no match for Marv, I'd come to love the game itself, its geometry and simple physicality. I picked off the ten on a long corner shot and set up the nine for an easy bank into the side pocket. The next shot was a combo. The fourteen rolled in.

Pool was often the best part of our time together, the quiet companionship around the table, something risen from the ashes of our acrobatic partnership all those years ago. Long after we'd left the bar, my mind and body would relive shots from our games, the memory of them still in my muscles.

The twelve rolled in and the bald man at the bar said, "Hot damn," and clapped once, twice, three times, slow and heavy. I allowed myself a quick glance. He was off his stool, chin down against his chest and hands ready to clap again. "Finish that up then lets play doubles"

"Against who?" Marv said.

"Me and Froggy. The old geezers. You guys'll wipe the floor with us."

I looked at Marv. "Froggy?" I mouthed. Marv gave a twitch of a smile and I returned to my shot. With a little top spin, the thirteen off the four and into the side set up the eleven for the corner.

"No money involved here," the bald man said.

The other man from the bar was approaching. I tipped in the eleven while the men shook hands. I didn't bother getting involved. "Froggy your real name?" Marv said.

The man nodded and gave a big oval grin as though Marv had asked to see his teeth.

"Froggy don't say a whole lot," the bald man said.

I missed my next shot, then Marv cleared the solids and sank the eight.

The bald man clapped again, heavy and slow. "God damn you two can shoot pool."

While Marv wheeled over for his beer, Froggy crouched and put in four of my quarters.

"Us against you," the bald man said. "Or should we mix it up? Froggy's a shark, I'll tell you that right now." He gave us a wink and a shadow of a nod.

"First we need drinks," said Marv. "Except for my sister, on account of her being Mormon." He grinned at me with the constipated look he gets when being nasty.

"Charlene." The bald man raised a hand. "Same again all around."

"Except for the shot of vodka," I said.

"Except the vodka," he called.

The waitress looked up. "I heard her the first time."

"For real you're a Mormon?" The bald man jutted his chin my way. "Not that there's anything wrong with that."

"No," I said while Marv set to work on the table, sinking balls with deliberate ease. "He just likes to lie."

The bald man moved with a confidence that matched Marv's. His delicate fingers held the cue quiet and still for a long slow beat before each shot. The moment the balls rolled, he was moving again, lining up the next one.

We narrowed it down to the eight ball and Marv sank it on a long, straight shot. Froggy racked and we played again.

Second game, I pocketed three balls in a row then missed a corner shot, but Marv pulled it off—he took the eight on a beautiful bank with an empty table. He spun around, made his eyes pop out a little. It's a trick he's been doing since grade five or six. The bald man stooped, levelled his face with Marv's. "Do that again and we'll be playing pool with your eyeballs."

Marv did it again. The bald man slapped Froggy's arm. "Will you look at that."

Marv faced the bar. "Celebrate with another round?"

The bald man pointed at me. "Sure you don't want to join us?"

I raised my mug. I don't drink around Marv. I'm trying to set an example, or at least trying not to encourage him. It's a rule I've set myself.

Marv picked up the chalk. "While she's fixing the drinks, lets play a quick singles game."

The bald man broke and I went to the washroom. A picture of Scarlet O'Hara marked the women's—a postcard sized shot, faded and wrinkled in one corner. As I locked the door, there was an out burst of laughter. I tilted my head and listened a moment. Muted voices, nothing more.

It always amazes me how quickly I can become the third wheel around Marv. It's men he talks to; men he connects with. There's a lot of Sundays I'm just a chauffeur.

When I returned, Marv was lining up a shot and the bald man was perched on a stool, one foot on a rung, the other dangling free. The waitress had fresh drinks on the table and a new pair of creamers sat beside my refilled mug. I took a stool in front of a Coors Light poster: three women in bikinis lying poolside.

Marv made his shot. The cue ball kissed the eight, nudged it into the pocket. Marv rolled away from the table and turned towards us. "Somebody rack."

"You'll notice no one's paid for drinks since I came over," the bald man said. "And much as The House would like to keep buying drinks all day, lets do this." He edged forward on his stool, paused as if to be sure he had Marv's full attention. "Best of five. Winner picks up the tab."

Marv raised his chin and scratched at the stubble on his neck. The bald man patted his shoulder. "How about some fun there Boy-o."

"Go ahead. Rack 'em."

At the far side of the table, the bald man fed in quarters. The table's fluorescent lights shone off the crown of his head. "Set us up, Froggy."

"This isn't part of the deal," I said at last.

"Deal?"

"You know, Marv, the deal. Our deal."

He rolled to the end of the table and began chalking his cue. "You go on about how badly I manage money. You should be happy I'm getting him to pay our drinks. Yours too."

"That's not what you're doing." My words though were low and aimed into my coffee. Marv backed up to the head of the table. "We should go soon. It's almost three."

"You're like a married couple, you two."

Marv broke. The balls scattered. I walked down to the jukebox. Next to it hung half a dozen old photographs—Southern soldiers staring out through time. Most were of distant figures under sprawling skies, their faces shadowed under wide-brimmed hats. One was a portrait, a close up of a boy with matted hair, a clean face and hollow cheeks, dark sunken eyes. His lips made a thin straight line. He was a skeleton wrapped in skin. He held a large knife, but no other weapon.

On the jukebox, I chose three songs by Neil Young, despite the fact it might annoy Marv. I picked "Southern Man" just to see if I could annoy anyone else.

The songs came on one after another while the pool balls rolled. Marv didn't complain about Neil Young's whine. He didn't even seem to notice. He rolled to the near side of the table and lined up a shot. The cue ball hit with a crack and the six slid into the corner pocket. Marv rolled forward and set up another.

To understand my brother and me, picture a mountain range,

a geography of sharp edges—no plateaus, no level meadows. Of course it hasn't always been this way. In those years we performed together, our bodies intertwined five days a week during afternoon practice. He was my base, our bodies aligned so he was like an extension of myself. Every sinew and muscle, every sharp point of bone familiar to me.

Our best skills were in the tempo routine. Two and a half minutes, every movement synchronized. Pitched tuck, catch and re-catch. A sharp lift then the overhead boosted somersault. I was light and trim and for a fraction of a second I could fly. It's been six years, but those moments of tumbling flight are still etched into my body.

The games chalked up on the board. A game for Marv, one for the bald man. It went past five games and the drinks kept coming. Froggy was keeping track on the board. Charlene was keeping track at the cash register. I kept track on my watch.

Halfway into the seventh game, I promised myself I'd interrupt when it ended. Problem was, Marv was behind. He could hardly afford to pay for his own drinks, let alone cover the whole tab. So I kept silent while Froggy set them up again and Charlene brought over another round.

Marv broke while my fingernails worried the seam of my jeans.

At the end of the game, I said, "Look Marv, four o'clock. Time to go."

"Will you give me a fucking break. We're just getting into it."

"It's four o'clock."

"Little Lady's right. We're past five games. Froggy, what's the situation?"

We all knew the bald man was up. Each game was a neatly drawn chalk line.

The bald man extended a hand to Marv. "You're one hell of a pool player. I'll get Charlene to total it up."

"Hell of a pool player yourself. After we had money on the game."

"Now listen, Marv. I don't want you to feel that way. This is just covering the tab is all."

"You and fucked-up Froggy drinking on me all day."

"More than half the bill is you. I had three beers tops—"

"Moment we came in here, you had your eye on us."

"I don't want you to feel bad about this, Marv. I like you. You're a great guy. Bet's a bet, though."

He started for the bar, where Charlene was putting bags of chips into a rack.

"Never bet on pool with strangers," Charlene said.

"Will you shut the fuck up," Marv said.

I reached for my jacket. "Come on, Marv. I'll pay for my coffees."

"Double or nothing," my brother called.

The bald man stopped and turned. His wiry eyebrows arched. "Charlene, what are we at on the tab?"

"Sixty-seven bucks." She raised a slip of paper. "Not that anyone's listening to me about betting on pool."

"That would make it 134, which is a chunk of change."

"I can add, Buddy." Marv pointed his cue at the table. "Play pool."

"Marvin, don't be stupid," I said, and immediately regretted the choice of words.

Marv's head cocked. He squinted at me then turned away. Nothing I could say would get him out now. I tried, though. I said: "It's late, and I have to run."

"So, go." He wheeled towards the table. "Rack 'em Froggy."

The bald man hefted up his pants and walked past me. "Well this is your choice, Marvin, that's all I'm saying. There's no pressure here."

"One game. All in."

The bald man dug into his pocket and set four quarters on the table. Froggy put them in the slots, licked his lips and set the balls free.

"Turns out you're a real player, Marv. But just to be clear, how will you be paying?"

Marv pulled out his wallet, fingered through it, and produced a credit card.

"Jesus Christ, Marvin."

The bald man walked the card to Charlene. "Could we take plastic?"

"Depends if you're planning to pay down your own tab."

I crouched in front of Marv and gripped his chair. "Marv," I said. "Please."

"Wait in the parking lot. I'll be out in five."

"The deal is we come for two hours and then we go."

"Will you stop it with your fucking deals, Lisa."

He wheeled away, shrugging and pulling at his shirt as though trying to get comfortable in it again. I headed straight for the door, walked without looking back.

"Five minutes," he yelled. "Just five God-damned minutes."

Outside, the sun had broken through and the brightness gave me pause. I stood there, gazing at the overexposed world and letting my eyes adjust.

In the car, I rolled the dial to the CBC, then started the engine. For a while I let it idle—wanting to put it in gear but knowing it wasn't in me. I laid my head against the driver's side window, switched off the engine, and wished I could cry.

Dixie's door finally opened, and the bald man stepped out. He helped Marv down the one step.

I stood by the car while my brother rolled over. He shifted from his chair into the passenger seat, then pushed the chair back and slammed his door. I folded the chair, set it in the trunk, and shut the lid as hard as I could.

Marv twisted, watched over his shoulder while I returned to the driver's side.

We pulled into traffic and I promised myself I'd keep quiet—I'd seethe and stew in it, but I wouldn't show an interest in his mess.

Two blocks down Dufferin, he asked for my phone. I pointed to it on the dash. He punched in a number from something in his wallet. For a while he was on hold and gazed out the passenger window at the fading residue of the afternoon rain. "Fucking hustler," he said.

"Marvin, you know what?"

"Hello." He plugged his other ear. "I'd like to report my credit card stolen."

"Marv."

I reached for the phone. "Give me that." He leaned away. He pushed at me with his free hand and the car swerved. I swatted at him. The phone fell into his lap, but he snatched it back up. "Just God damn drive." He put the phone to his other ear and leaned away.

"Marvin," I yelled.

"Hello. Are you still there? Hello? Fuck." He threw the phone onto the dash. "Fuck! Thanks a fuck." He smashed a fist into the glove box, pushed at the door then looked back out the passenger window.

"What are you doing with your life, Marvin? I mean what the hell—"

"—Will you shut it? Will you please for one God-damned second get off my back."

"Off your back? Is that what you want?"

"Yes, that's what I want. That's exactly what I want."

"All right then." I slowed the car, signalled and pulled over. "I will get off your back."

As the car came to a halt, Marv banged on the dash. "Let me out of this fucking rattle trap."

Tears were on their way. They were rising slowly through my body. I leaned forward until my forehead touched the steering wheel. Where does a person go from here? Who's drawn the map for this?

He was banging against the door, against the dash. "Get my chair. I'm getting out."

I finally opened the driver's side, only instead of popping the trunk, I started walking. Behind me he was yelling, calling my name. Down the side walk stood a row of newspaper boxes spray painted red and black. A woman sat on a milk crate.

At the corner the lights changed. Traffic stopped and started. Cars sped by. Above me, the control box clicked. Birds circled. Clouds moved, hurried on by winds from the north.

In the distance now, my brother called my name. I took a deep breath, turned and began to walk. When I reached the Oldsmobile, I opened the trunk, pulled out my brother's chair and set it on the sidewalk, open and waiting for him.

∼

Marv and Darren arrived late. They didn't get to the party until almost midnight and things were already petering out. The music was still blaring, but the only person they could see from the hallway was passed out on the sofa—her arms spread wide as if awaiting a hug. Marv led the way past her and into the living room where a guy was dancing alone in front of the fireplace, body undulating as though rocked by waves from below. "Check out Dancing Boy." Darren had to yell to be heard over the music. "Just so you know, this girl, Melanie, she hangs out with lots of art fags."

Dancing Boy turned a little. His tee shirt was skin tight. It showed every ripple of flesh, every taut muscle. Marv tried not to stare, but watching that body, a pressure built inside, a pressure that rose through his chest seeking relief.

Dancing Boy began moving faster. He had a way of shimmying his entire upper body. All this time he had his eyes closed. He was in his own world.

A girl rushed into the room, wrapped both arms around Darren, hug and release. Marv lingered a few steps off, noticed a girl in the corner who was also dancing. From the shadows of the music, a voice emerged, a low moan that ground up through the melody while a heavier beat rose to push the music forward. Just then Dancing Boy opened his eyes and looked straight at Marv. For a brief moment he stopped dancing and stared, chest rising and falling, still catching his breath. Marv turned away.

"Mel, this is my buddy Marv," Darren yelled.

Marv stepped forward. Melanie had big curly hair and horn-rimmed glasses which she might have been wearing as a joke. "Where is everybody?" Marv said. "Where's the keg?"

"Keg?" she shouted.

Marv batted a hand at her. The music was too loud to try and make a joke. He gave a beer drinking gesture. She pointed and Marv headed towards what he assumed was the kitchen.

Marv didn't know Melanie. He didn't know anybody here. This whole outing was Darren's idea. They'd left a perfectly good party, walked half an hour in below freezing temperatures to join in what seemed like aftermath.

Marv slipped past a girl in an Indian style leather jacket—beads, tassels, feathers and all. He watched her turn the corner, glanced again at Dancing Boy who had shuffled towards the centre of the room, moving faster now as the music shed its skin and sped forward. Marv squatted at the fridge. The top two shelves were filled with empty beer cases. He managed to fish two bottles from the back then returned to the living room. Darren and Melanie had disappeared. Dancing Boy had his back to him and Marv watched a while. The girl who'd been dancing in the corner was just standing still. She gave Marv a conspiratorial smile like she'd caught him starring, like she knew what he was thinking. Blush rising to his face, Marv returned to the kitchen. A guy with bleached blond hair had started making popcorn in a jiffy pan. In the fogged up window beside the stove, someone had drawn a heart shape.

The kitchen table was crowded with empties. Marv sat at the end by the fridge and took a long drink of beer. Even at this end of the house the music was loud. A woman's voice climbed over the tripping beat, rose to a pitch, almost a scream then stopped suddenly. A chorus of drums with a tribal sounding beat took up the

54

space. Marv took a swig of beer. Across the room, the girl in the leather jacket pointed at him. "I know you." She touched a finger to her temple. The jacket's tassels rippled while her finger held there as though to help generate memories. "Psychology with Maddox, right?"

"Of course." He nodded. "Right. Thought I recognized you too."

Her hair was all kinked, blond and turned into zigzags. She pushed a few strands from her face, extended a hand. "Billie," she said.

"Marv." They shook. It was a strangely formal moment. It made Marv straighten a little. "So where is everybody?" he said.

Billie looked around, shrugged. "Don't know. Gone home." The counter was a field of empties. On the floor, a pitcher of something blue had a beer can floating in it. There was a puddle on the lino in front of the sink.

Billie was smiling. She had a round face, wide eyes and a little ski jump nose. He was surprised he hadn't remembered her from class. "Love that jacket," he said at last. "Tassels. Beads. All that Indian stuff."

"Thrift shop special."

Marv reached out, knocked a tassel with his forefinger. It caused a tiny ripple of movement. "Spin around or something. Lets see the beads at work."

She spun and the tassels leapt to life. She moved so quickly she had to reach for the fridge to steady herself. "Whoa did I drink too much." She sat beside Marv, pushed hair from her face and set both elbows on the table. "When some girls get drunk, people take advantage of them. When others get drunk, people ignore them."

Marv managed a laugh. His thumbnail dug into the beer bottle's label. "So what's your major?"

Billie turned to look at him, held up a finger. "I don't talk about that."

"What, it's a secret?"

"People should talk about more important things. About their passions. What's really important. This is my beef—"

"—Okay. So what's your passion?"

"The theatre." She said it in a grand way, like she might have been poking fun at herself.

"Does that also happen to be your major?"

"Maybe."

"My buddy Darren said you were all kind of artsy here."

"And what's your passion, Marv?"

"Mine? Jesus Christ."

"No way." She slapped the table. "That's so trippy. For real?"

"No. That was totally a joke." He leaned his head back against the wall, suddenly tired, suddenly unsure why he was flirting, why he bothered heaping his attention on this girl. He finished his beer, opened the second bottle and glanced towards the living room. "Once thought I was going to the Olympics."

"Get out." She pushed at him and her hand lingered on his chest a moment. "In what?"

"Gymnastics."

"No wonder you're so buff. Make a muscle."

Marv shook his head. He tried to chuckle.

"Come on," Billie said, and suddenly Dancing Boy was there in the hall walking towards them. He had a chocolaty walk, smooth, rich, his whole body part of the effort. Billie followed Marv's gaze. "Steven." She stood, grabbed Dancing Boy's shoulder, wrapped him into a hug.

"Billie. Where did everyone go? Left me dancing all alone."

"That's awful. Come sit with us. Marv meet Steven, Steven meet Marv." Steven's thin lips tightened into a smile. He raised a hand and said something only the words were soft and the music was too loud.

"Want a beer?" Marv yelled.

Steven nodded.

Marv stood and walked to the fridge. He picked out two more. "I'm distributing other people's beer. Robin Hood meets Animal House."

Steven's hips swayed even while he was standing there. "You like to dance?" he said.

Marv nodded, and then it occurred to him that Steven might actually be asking him to dance. "I mean, sometimes," he said and drank from his beer, aware of the warmth of Steven's gaze across his body.

"He likes my jacket," Billie said.

"True. I like her jacket."

Steven plucked at the beads along one fringe.

"He's a gymnast." Billie pointed at Marv. "Ask him to do some moves."

"Was. A long time ago." Marv drank again. "Gave it up to do acrobatic gymnastics with my sister."

"Well no wonder you're so buff. Acrobatic gymnastics."

In an impulsive moment, in the glow of Steven's smile, Marv flexed an arm.

"Well, well," Steven said.

Billie pushed herself from the wall where she was leaning. "Washroom," she said and headed down the hall.

Steven started moving again, a ghost of a dance, a nod, a shift of one hip, picking up on odd bits of the music. And as he danced, he edged forward. "I like your shirt."

"This?" Marv plucked at the shirt, glanced down and Steven touched the sleeve, fingers flat as though to smooth it.

"Looks good on you."

Marv smiled. He nodded and for a moment his nod caught the music's beat. Nineteen, drunk in the house of a stranger, Marv stood at a threshold, ready and waiting to be pulled across. Steven stepped closer. For a moment Marv thought he could smell him, a cologne, a hint of perspiration. He took it all in, sucked it down deep into his core. And then Marv thought of Darren and he lost his breath. He stepped away, looked around the room, glanced back down the hallway, sweat suddenly beading under his arms.

"What?" Steven said. "Something wrong?"

Billie trotted back into the room and Marv could breath normally again. "There's puke all over the floor," she said. "I can't go anymore. Lets dance."

Steven turned to face Billie and as he moved, the back of his hand brushed Marv's thigh. Marv wanted to reach out, wanted to connect and return the discreet gesture, but his hand didn't cooperate. And what did it matter? This was a beginning not an end. He stood there, enjoying the rising tingling where Steven's hand had touched his thigh.

"Want to dance?"

"Sure," Marv said, but then he thought of Darren again and his mind churned over what Darren might say if he found Marv gyrating with Dancing Boy. "Just let me have a smoke first."

"Outside," Billie said. "You have to do it outside."

"It's freezing out there."

"Give him your jacket." Steven clapped. He looked pleased with himself. "It will look good on you. Lets see it."

Billie slipped it off. It was a bit small for Marv, short in the arms. He shifted about to make the tassels and beads move.

"Beautiful," Steven said and so Marv kept it on, followed the others down the hall. Marv took the cigarettes and lighter from Darren's coat by the door. He set one hand on the knob while Billie and Steven spun off into their own worlds, slipping into a trance-like, rhythmic sway. Steven danced with his eyes closed, his head turned down as though he wanted to be watched, as though to offer anonymity to any who wished to stare.

Two girls started dancing at the edge of the room. The music continued to rise, beat edging up through the melody with a renewed urgency. Marv stepped outside. He lit his cigarette, held in the smoke, felt himself go dizzy as he watched Steven through the window.

The door opened behind Marv. It was Billie. "Now you're going to want your jacket back."

"Not if you'll keep me warm." She wrapped an arm around him, pulled herself close.

"Do we even know each other?" he said, aware of the soft warmth of her breast against his ribs.

She raised her head, smiled. "Give me a smoke?"

Marv offered the pack. "They're not even mine. Don't really smoke much."

She lit up, inhaled deeply, and put her arm back around him. "If you're going to wear my jacket, you have to keep me warm."

"You're the one who wants to smoke out here in Siberia."

Marv gazed at the bare bulb above them. The filament seemed to quiver. He looked at it long enough that when he turned away, the shape of the filament remained on his retina.

"Did I tell you I was a mathematical genius when I was a child?" Billie said.

Marv tossed his cigarette. "Yeah, well I was an acrobatic gymnastics champion."

"Actually, I wasn't a mathematical genius. I was a royal pain in the ass. Only child. Ruled the roost."

"I think my sister ruled the roost." He looked through the window as he spoke, watched Steven gyrate and quiver. Every inch of Marv's body suddenly felt cold, like the wind had found its way through the stitches of his clothing.

"The girls usually do," Billie said.

For a moment Marv wasn't sure what she was talking about. He was busy wishing he hadn't taken her jacket, busy wishing he was warm in his own coat, wishing it was Steven out here standing so close.

"So," he said at last. "Dancing Boy in there. Steven," but then Billie leaned closer, craned her neck and kissed him. It ended as abruptly as it had started, and then, as though this had settled something, Billie set her head on Marv's shoulder. She loosened the arm around him. "Acrobatic Gymnastics," she said. "That's your passion."

"My sister's passion more than mine to be honest."

"Oh." Billie raised her cigarette. Marv glanced back into the house. Steven was dancing close to the window. He seemed to be looking out at them, watching. Marv stepped from Billie's grip. Instead of heading in, he hopped onto the porch rail. Part of it was covering for his sudden movement, part of it was the inspiration of Steven's gaze. "Did you know men don't do balance beam for fear of injuring their testicles."

She snorted a laugh. Marv walked across the rail. It was about eight feet long, five inches wide with a slight bevel. He walked back to one end and dipped, alternating feet, did a waltz step getting a sense of the rail. At the end, he turned, spun 180 degrees. Facing the house, he looked straight at Steven who was close enough to the window that fog showed on the pane. For a long beat, they gazed at each other. "Straight jump, half turn," Marv said and did one across the beam. The jacket was a little constricting, but he executed without trouble. "Step leap," he said and returned.

Billie clapped, cigarette clamped between fingertips. "Bravo," she said.

In the window, Steven was nodding, narrow eyes focused on Marv. Facing the house again, with his back to the pillar, Marv spread his arms. "And dismount." He turned towards the snowy lawn and leapt.

The flip wasn't fully committed. He hesitated, some distant atoms in his body unsure. Perhaps his footing slipped, perhaps the jacket hindered his arms, perhaps the alcohol had marred his judgement or lack of practice had reduced his strength. In the air, the realization that he didn't get enough power flashed through his mind. And then he was on the ground. Here his memory falters. The night until that point remained vivid for the rest of his life, but he would never recall the pain of landing, the jerk of his body, what Billie later described as a bounce. He would never remember the way he called out, a moan more than anything. Nor would he ever recall the sudden rush of cold, nor Billie's screams and shrieks, wild beasts there in the snow. And he would never remember the way she and Steven each held a hand, warming his chilled fingers as the sound of a distant siren grew louder.

FLORIDA

Hal was waiting on the porch when his sister pulled in. He walked down the gravel drive to meet her and when he was close enough, snatched the keys from her hand. "We need bread and milk and all that." He slipped past her, opened the driver's door and climbed into the truck.

"You have enough money?" she said before he had a chance to close the door.

Hal patted his pockets. "Right, right. Money. How much you got on you?"

"How are you going shopping without money?" Suzie extended a hand. "Give me the keys, Hal."

"Forget it, Suzie. It's okay."

"Come on, Hal."

He pulled the door closed, locked it before she reached him. Suzie slapped the window while Hal mouthed bye-bye. She kept banging though and eventually Hal lowered it a crack. "Calm down," he said. "You're going to give yourself an asthma attack."

"Hal, will you just." Suzie closed her eyes and took a breath. "Please get out of my truck."

He started the engine and eased away from Suzie. He backed down the lane then at the highway, turned east towards town.

The vinyl seat was still wet with Suzie's sweat and Hal tried to keep his back from it. He rolled down the window then adjusted the rearview mirror and looked at himself. He ran a hand through his hair, gave a grin to check his teeth. He should have showered and shaved before leaving.

After the first set of lights, the road added a lane and traffic thickened. Hal passed a pair of motels, a grocery store, then a row of car dealerships. At a light near the mall, he found himself across from a knot of girls in short skirts clutching shopping bags. He eased the truck forward to get a better view, but then the light was green and he was moving again. It was the early dusk of spring's first hot night. Springsteen was on the radio. Hal was driving fast. He turned up the music.

At Quickie Mart, Hal slowed to an ant's pace and peered inside to figure out who was working. The girl at the counter wasn't Jean or the fat one. He parked, then walked back to the Mart's big window and watched the girl on duty. She was bent over the counter, backside waving at him through the glass. He opened the door and the buzzer sounded.

"Suzie sent me over for smokes."

The girl turned.

"Marlboro Lights. Good old Virginia tobacco. You know Suzie and the heat. She's sitting in front of the AC already."

The girl bent to get the cigarettes. "Suzie Ransom?" she said.

"Course Suzie Ransom. Does the morning shifts. You must be new here. I'm Hal. Suzie's brother." He extended a hand. "Came up from Florida for the funeral, and, you know." He shrugged.

"Oh, right. I was sorry to hear about your mother."

Hal nodded. "Thanks." He drummed his fingers on the counter. "You know what, make it two packs. I don't want to have to come back. Been running Suzie errands all day, I swear." He chuckled, and the girl bent for another pack. Her skirt spread tight against her backside.

"Anything else?"

"How late you working?"

The girl didn't answer that. The loose skin of her upper arms swung as she worked the cash register.

"Hold on," Hal said. "They're for her. Put them on her tab. They're not mine. Take it off her pay cheque. That's what they normally do."

"Well that's not really allowed."

Hal gave a wave. "You'll get used to it." He opened the door and the buzzer obscured whatever the girl said next.

Back in the truck, Hal balled up the cellophane from his cigarettes and dropped it out the window. He revved the engine, put the truck in gear, and lurched forward. The truck cleared the car parked in front just as a boy on a bike rode past. Hal's bumper clipped the back wheel, and the kid went over his handlebars, hit the pavement and rolled. Hal slammed on the brakes. He killed the engine and was out of the truck in a snap. He stepped over the bike, took the kid by the arm and helped him up.

"I'm okay," the kid said, but his whole body was trembling. Hal crouched. The boy wouldn't look at him though. He was bending his knees as though to make sure they still worked.

Across the street, an elderly lady in a flower print dress stared.

"Got a problem?" Hal shouted.

An oncoming car slowed as the driver watched Hal and the kid.

"So you're okay and all?" Hal asked.

The kid was still looking down at the cracked concrete beneath his feet. He nodded. "Yup. Okay." His voice was thin and high. A tear trickled down his cheek. He wiped it away with the back of his sleeve.

"Look, no biggie. We should just be glad it wasn't worse. Riding like that could make you dog food."

The boy didn't answer. Hal nudged him. "You want a ride home or something? Where you live at?"

"Just stings," the kid said, and finally he looked up at Hal. He had big eyes, brown and wide, almost liquid.

"You'll be okay in a few minutes, but you did a number on the bike." Hal tried to spin the rear wheel, but it was too warped to turn. "Listen, I got to go. You want a ride or not?" The kid had started to tremble again. "Where's home at?"

"Drummond." The kid pointed.

"You direct. I'll drive." Hal set the bike in the flatbed and walked back to where the front end of the truck still poked into the street. He got his smokes off the seat just before the kid slid inside.

They took the first corner and the next. Hal was trying to get headed where the boy had pointed. At the second stop sign, he lit up. He thought of offering a cigarette, but the kid couldn't have been more than eleven or twelve. No point in giving him one if he didn't really want it. Hal rested his elbow on the window and blew a stream of smoke across the steering wheel. "You ever think of getting a helmet? They might look stupid, but all the kids wear them. It's probably even the law."

"I know."

Hal was at an intersection. "You going to tell me where to go?"

The kid pointed.

"How far?"

The boy shrugged. "Further down."

Hal watched him a moment before making the turn. He had freckles, wide constellations of them across both cheeks. His mouth hung open in a strange way. It occurred to Hal the kid might be a little retarded. "You don't talk a whole lot. Cat got your tongue?"

"I guess." And then in the next breath the kid said, "Are you religious?" He pointed to the statue of the Virgin Mary glued to the dash.

Hal pulled the statue off. He tossed it on the floor. "Like that when I bought the truck." He flicked his cigarette butt out the window.

"Are you Indian?"

"Indian?" Hal said. "What the fuck are you talking about?"

The kid shrugged.

"I'm not Indian. I'm Polish. Italian. Whatever." He glanced at the kid a moment. "If you're talking about the hella tan, it's just a lot of time at the beach. I live in Florida. The Sunshine State. Man, the chicks in Florida. I mean, you would not believe the chickitas." He slapped the steering wheel and leaned a little closer. "Bikini is formal dress in Fort Lauderdale, if you know what I'm saying."

The boy was staring straight ahead. His mouth was still hanging open. "My cousin's Indian," he said.

"What d'you mean your cousin's Indian?"

Hal waited. No answer.

"Wouldn't that make you Indian?"

"My uncle's Indian but my aunt isn't."

"Right. Okay. It's like by marriage."

At the next light, Hal noticed the girl driving next to them. She looked his way a moment. Hal tried to catch her eye, but she pulled ahead and made a right turn. "That mean your cousin can get me cheap smokes?"

"It's not by marriage," the kid said. "You can't be Indian by marriage. You're born Indian or—"

"—All right, all right. Enough about the Indian thing. Jesus." Hal hung his arm out the window and drummed on the door panel. "Where do we turn?"

"Mackenzie."

"Okay. Mackenzie."

"It's back there."

"Back?" Hal hit the breaks. "Why the fuck didn't you tell me?"

"Forgot."

"You're supposed to tell me where we're going. I live in Florida, remember. Jesus. How far back?"

"By the gas station."

Hal waited for a break in the traffic, pulled a U-turn. He couldn't remember any gas stations. "No yackking," he said. "Just tell me when to turn." It was almost eight o'clock. It was time to get on with the night. "I got business to take care of. I mean, Jesus Christ, I'm a busy man. I got business tonight, you know."

"What kind of business?"

"My own business."

"Like a store?"

"Would you just focus please? It's time to focus."

"My dad's going into business."

After about a mile, they passed a PetroCan then a Shell. Hal glanced over. The kid shook his head. "Maybe you could tell my dad about doing business?"

"Me?" Hal said.

The boy nodded.

"Your dad wants to know about business? About how to make money?"

He nodded again.

"All right," he said. "Find something that's been done already and do it better. That's basically it. Find an idea and steal it. Copying is how you make money. Plus you go where the money is. And it isn't up here in Asswipe, Ontario, believe me."

"Here," the kid said. It was a narrow side street. No trees, just squat houses in tight rows. A couple of street lights bathed the road ahead. "Drummond's at the end."

Hal parked in front of the boy's place. It was a low concrete affair. The lights from the house cast white squares across a patchy lawn. The kid didn't move to get out. "So what's your name anyways?"

"Shawn."

Hal extended his hand. "Good to meet you, Shawn. How do you like the door-to-door service?"

"Good," the kid said, but he still didn't move to get out.

"Well, you leaving or you moving in?"

"What sort of business are you doing tonight?"

"Business? It's just an expression. I got things to do. I'm not like a travelling salesman or something."

"Oh."

"I actually came up for my mother's funeral. I was just here for that and now I'm back down to the Sunshine State."

"Oh, okay."

66

"Kid, you don't just say 'Oh, okay'. That's not what you say when someone reports that his mother died. You say 'I'm sorry to hear that.'"

"I'm sorry to hear that," Shawn said.

"Forget it. No big deal. If you believe her, she went straight to Heaven on account of going to church every Sunday."

Hal reached out and rolled his finger on the radio dial, sent it one way then the other. "Cancer's an awful way to go," he said. "Don't ever smoke."

Above them, the light was slipping from the sky. The setting sun cast a pink haze across a bank of clouds. "One day I was down in sunny Florida then my sister phoned and next day I was up here. Got on the first flight."

"So how did you get the truck here?"

Hal shifted in his seat, pushed back against the springs like he needed more space. "Bought it just for while I'm up actually. I'll maybe give it to my sister when I leave. She hasn't got two pennies to rub together." Hal looked out at the little bungalow, its drawn curtains, and the soft light beyond. "Me, I got a drop-top Caddy. Use it to cruise the chicks on Ocean Drive. I like the good life. Penthouse suite on Miami Beach. Good food. Lots of girls. In America, you got to be rich to be anyone."

"Oh."

"Don't even know why I came, really. We weren't particularly close. Plus she died before I arrived. And she left everything to my sister and the church."

"Was she Catholic?" Shawn pointed at the little statue now lying on the floor.

"Now I'm just kicking around, waiting for what to do next. They might not even let me back across the border."

"What about the penthouse and your Caddy?"

"What is this, twenty questions, for Christ sakes?"

A toddler had waddled onto the porch. A large woman followed, hair in curlers, cigarette in hand. She folded her arms and

67

stood watching. Hal waved. He got out, walked around and lowered the tailgate.

"What's going on here?" The woman's voice was as big as her belly. It was a voice honed by years of yelling at kids.

"This your boy?" Hal asked. "Ran into me over by Quickie Mart. He's okay. Only scrapes. Nothing to worry about. Got to start wearing a helmet, though."

The woman ambled down to the sidewalk, haunches moving her dress with each step. Hal set the bike on the ground. He could feel the woman's gaze crawling across him.

She set a hand on Shawn's head. "Not watching where you're going, Junior?" She didn't look at the kid as she spoke. She was still watching Hal. "Huh? You not looking where you're going?"

Shawn mumbled something.

Hal slammed the tailgate and walked around to the driver's side. Back on the sidewalk, the woman cuffed Shawn hard enough to turn his head around. "Don't get in a car with a stranger. Men like that." She flicked ash towards the truck but didn't continue. Hal waved, turned the key. The engine coughed once, twice, then died. "And you." The woman peered at Hal through the windscreen. "I got your licence plate, Mister."

Hal waved, while turning the key with his other hand. The engine caught. He revved it and pulled out.

Hal found his way back onto Simpson and followed a trickle of traffic north towards the highway, past the mall and the liquor store. For a while he just smoked and drove, not even sure where he was in the tangle of growth north of town: new roads, new developments, new strip malls and warehouses, four lane roads, box stores, parking lots. By nine o'clock, he found himself heading west on 17. He killed the lights as he pulled into his sister's place, cut the engine and cruised up her lane in silence.

The moment the door banged closed, Suzie asked what kind of milk he'd bought. "I told you I'm broke," Hal said. "We've been over this already."

"You just drove around wasting my gas?"

Hal collapsed into the arm chair, kicked it back, and pulled out a cigarette. "You got enough gas up your ass you don't need to worry."

"Whose cigarettes?" Suzie said.

"Yours."

"Mine?"

"Yours and mine." He tossed what was left of the pack onto the coffee table. It slid halfway across.

"You didn't take them from the Mart?"

"No, I didn't take them. You can't just take cigarettes."

"You didn't do that thing where you tell them to bill me?"

Hal didn't answer.

"You son of a bitch. I'm going to lose my job."

"No you won't."

"I will. Frank finds out, I'm toast." She ran both hands through her hair. "You got to take them back. Right now."

"I can't. The pack's half gone."

"Buy another."

"You go buy another." Hal lit up, blew smoke towards the ceiling. "What are you watching?"

Suzie threw the remote at him. It hit the armchair. She threw a pillow and then a plastic tray. Hal sheltered himself with his arms.

"Suzie, for Christ sake."

"I'll lose my job. Frank said that last time."

"Calm down. You'll give yourself an asthma attack." He took the other pack from his shirt pocket. "Take this."

"Another? You took two?" She pointed at the door. "Get out."

Hal laughed. He covered his mouth. "I'm sorry, okay? All right?"

"Out."

"At least wait until this show's over." It was *America's Funniest Home Videos*. A cat had just fallen into a bath tub.

"You better listen," Suzie yelled. She picked up a hockey stick. "A month you been sitting on your ass."

Suzie hit the arm chair. It shuddered. She hit it again and again. She swung until she was wheezing and coughing.

Hal raised a hand. "If you actually hit me, I'll hit you back."

Suzie didn't let up, though. The vibrations came through with each connection. And then one swing fell short and caught Hal on the shoulder. An arrow of pain shot into his chest. His fingers went numb. He doubled over, his right hand instinctively cradling his arm.

"Oh my God!" Suzie cried. She dropped the hockey stick. "I'm sorry, Harold. I didn't mean it."

Hal managed to stand. He began walking.

"You don't have to go, Hal. It's okay."

Hal kept walking, though. At the doorway, he lifted his arm, rotated it a little, slowly exploring the pain, then he headed down the steps and into the night. Behind him the door banged shut.

Hal felt his pockets. The keys were still there. He set a hand on the warm hood of the truck. The dog star was bright in the sky and low to the south. He could hop in the truck and follow that star all the way to Florida. He moved around to the driver's side and opened the door. The statute of the Virgin Mary still lay on the floor.

Hal lay across the bench seat, his head against the armrest. He propped the statue on his chest. It rose and fell with his breathing but remained upright. He could feel the keys digging into his thigh, but Hal knew he'd go no further. He swallowed, and licked his lips.

"I," he said, directing his attention to the little statue. He took a deep breath and his mind struggled for what came next.

Stopping for Strangers

My sister and I were on our way to see Grandfather one last time before he died. Sheri had brought a copy of the Bible to read him. She knew he'd be too far gone to hear, but he was a religious man. He had copies of the Bible all over the house. If he'd known what she was doing, he'd have appreciated it.

I hadn't brought anything to read, hadn't planned out what I'd say, hadn't even thought a lot about the fact that this was good-bye. The trip was Sheri's idea, and it was more her trip than mine. Although I did pull over for the hitch hiker, and that turned out to be more important than it had seemed at the time.

We'd just switched drivers when I spotted the kid. It was raining and he had his jacket pulled over his head. I signaled and edged onto the shoulder. He ran to catch up, and when he got into the car he was panting. The door slammed. I accelerated, pulled back onto the highway and the kid said thanks, said he was going to Trenton. He took off his jacket, leaned between the front seats and that's when he noticed the Bible on Sheri's lap. "Hey." He rolled up one sleeve, got the cuff up above his elbow and stuck out his forearm. He had a cross tattoo, black and about three inches long. "I'm a Christian too."

He held still for a moment, fist clenched on the arm rest be-tween Sheri and me. None of us spoke and the kid eventually shifted back, did up his safety belt. "I'm trying not to get your seat too wet back here."

Sheri twisted around to face him. "Mind if I ask how old you are?"

"Sixteen." Gum smacked between his teeth.

"You're sixteen and you have a tattoo?"

"Got three." He unbuttoned his shirt, angled his shoulder forward. There was a flash of tattooed flesh in the rearview mirror. He lowered his shirt further to show something on his chest. "Mom signed the release, said I could get the eagle if I also got the cross. This other one my buddy's brother did." I adjusted the rearview mirror to get a better look. He was pointing to a ring tattooed on his chest. "Circle of life." He spat the wad of gum into his hand, rolled down the window and tossed it out.

The rain had slowed by the time we turned off at Trenton. A doughnut shop lay within sight of the highway. I pulled up in front of the plate glass window. The kid said goodbye, God bless, then ran for shelter. We watched until he was inside. Sheri's fingers drummed the Bible. "Doughnuts," she said. "My former favourite food."

"Just say if you want one."

She shook her head, and I eased the car out of the lot and headed for the highway.

We pulled back into traffic, and Sheri said, "Hope you're not missing any important classes."

"No. None."

Truth was I hadn't been going to many classes. It was too late to get money back, so I hadn't officially quit, and I hadn't really told anyone. I'd been mulling over how to tell Sheri ever since she'd picked me up in North York. Now seemed a good time to get it out in the open, only just then Sheri noticed the case in the back seat. She reached for it. "The kid forgot his glasses." She snapped it open. "Oh shit. Diabetes." She showed me the needle. "We should go back."

"I don't know. He'll probably be gone by now." We were already three or four miles down the 401.

"It'll only take ten minutes."

That seemed optimistic. My mind tried to do the math.

"Mark, he needs his medication."

I signaled as we approached the next exit.

"Thank you," she said and we headed back in silence. The conversation about university was buried now, and I didn't revive it. I already knew what Sheri would say. We came from a well-educated family. Sheri alone had two degrees, and she was only three years older than me. The family had expectations.

By the time we got back to the doughnut shop, the rain had stopped entirely. Through the plate glass windows I could see he was gone. I switched off the engine. Sheri ran in. She talked to the woman behind the counter, raised the case, nodded and backed off a step. She spoke to a couple near the door then came back out.

"No luck?" I said.

"His address is under the lining. 419 Medical. Name is Tim Mundson." She rattled the case. I started the engine. "It's not far."

We followed the doughnut woman's directions, headed south on Glen Miller Road, under railroad tracks, past a mall then turned into a development of small houses on large plots, little boxes evenly spaced. A car approached us, pulled into a lane beside a truck perched on concrete blocks.

We paused at the next intersection. Beside us, close to the road, stood a rusty swing set. I strained to read the street sign. Although it was only four o'clock, the light was fading, and it felt like dusk.

Medical turned out to be the second to last block. 419 sat on the edge of fields. Its roof was a patchwork of green and black shingles. The verandah tilted into the side yard and the grey paint on the clapboard was peeling badly.

"Lovely," Sheri said.

I cut the engine, and we looked at each other. Sheri was biting her nails.

At first glance, Sheri is all cautious conservatism. She keeps things in order. Her house is always tidy. At nineteen she bought her first RRSP. But she also has an impulsive streak. It wouldn't have surprised me if she'd thought of that RRSP in the morning and bought it that afternoon. She might even have had second thoughts that evening. That's the way she operates. Impulse and second thoughts. Nail biting indicated second thoughts.

"I'll do it." I reached for the case, but she pulled it away and opened her door. Both of us walked to the porch. Sheri rang the bell.

In the field beyond the house, tall grass bent in the wind. Further west the sky was clearing. A slice of blue had broken through the stacks of clouds, a long bright arm just above the horizon.

There was a noise behind the door. The light switched on above us and the door opened.

"Is Tim in? Tim Mundson?"

The woman folded her arms and dropped her chin. It made her ponytail bob. "Timmy?" she said. "You want Timmy?" She was plump and her cheeks rose a little as she spoke.

Sheri raised the case. "We've got his insulin needle. He was hitch hiking. We dropped him off at the doughnut store a few minutes ago, saw this and his address inside."

"Oh well, well." Her voice rose warm and high. "Come on in then."

Sheri held out the case, but the woman didn't notice. She was already two steps into the kitchen. Her ponytail brushed the nape of her neck as she moved.

"Allen, we got visitors," she yelled and then she motioned for us to come in. "Timmy's not home just yet."

The door swung closed. I wiped my boots.

"Allen's my eldest. Just back from Rwanda." She bent and collected something from a cupboard. "Coffee or tea?"

"We should probably be on our way," I said, but Allen was thumping down the stairs and it obscured my words. He stood for a moment on the bottom step. He had a short crop of black hair and bushy eyebrows. He didn't look much like the kid we'd picked up. Except for the haircut, he didn't look much like a soldier either.

"Come on and talk to these people," Mrs. Mundson said. "They just gave Timmy a ride then found out he'd left his insulin."

Sheri raised the case, held it out, but Mrs. Mundson ignored her again. She was pouring water into the coffee maker. Allen didn't move for the case either. Sheri set it on the counter.

"I don't like to think of Timmy hitch hiking," Mrs. Mundson said. "It's okay when someone like you picks him up, but I don't know." She set a pair of mugs on the counter, pulled down two more. "Why don't you have a seat there? Take a load off. Coffee's already on."

I was ready to say we should go. My hand was still on the doorknob, but Sheri bent and slipped off her shoes.

A sofa and two arm chairs faced each other on a square of carpet at the far end of the room. Sheri and I sat on the sofa. Mrs. Mundson took one arm chair, and Allen perched on the arm of the other. Seeking something to occupy my attention, I lifted a photo from the end table. It was Mrs. Mundson and Allen with another woman and a boy I didn't recognize.

"That's the family. Plus my sister," Mrs. Mundson said. "Timmy was awful chubby that summer, wasn't he, Allen?"

Sheri had her coffee at her lips. She didn't seem to notice the picture I was studying. The boy in it wasn't the one we'd picked up. It wasn't Tim we'd given a lift from Port Hope, but I didn't say anything, just set the picture back where I'd found it.

Allen cracked his knuckles. One hand then the other, the hollow pop of strained joints.

"When I heard the bell," Mrs. Mundson said. "I thought you were the Mormons. They come by here just about every Thursday, don't they Allen? Ever since he went to Rwanda. I was good as alone all the time. `Course once I saw you, I knew you weren't Mormons."

I lifted my mug. A painted Cinderella smiled from its surface. As I took a sip, Allen said, "That thing in your mouth hurt when you eat and kiss and that?" Sheri coughed. I had trouble keeping down my mouthful. He was talking about my lip ring.

"Mind your manners." Mrs. Mundson reached out and tapped her son's arm, but Allen was gazing into his mug. He smiled to himself.

"He's just like that sometimes," Mrs. Mundson said. "Hey Allen, go get them one of your little carvings to say thank you."

Allen looked up at her, but he didn't say anything. Sheri said not to bother. "We have to go in a minute." She batted a hand his way and took a big gulp of coffee.

"Oh, he's got a ton of them," Mrs. Mundsen said. "And he's trying to sell them, aren't you, Allen? This might drum you up some business."

Allen shrugged.

"Go on," she said. "Go on up there."

Allen set down his coffee and headed for the stairs.

"He bought all these little carvings over there in Africa," Mrs. Mundsen said. "More than you could stand in a room. Little carved heads and that." As Allen thumped up the stairs, she lowered her voice. "He bought them all with Canadian Tire money. Got me to send him wads of it. All them people he was trading with were so ignorant they thought they were getting rich."

I tried to catch Sheri's eye, but she was watching Mrs. Mundson. My finger toyed with a loose thread from the sofa.

"He said he was going to open a store, but half the signalmen did the same thing and Trenton's overrun with all sorts of little African whatnots."

I stood up then, thinking we should go, wanting to stretch my legs. Sheri didn't move. There was a thud upstairs. I looked up at the ceiling.

"Why don't you go on up and see them too? It's something else."

"That's all right. I'll just take a look at what he brings down."

"Allen?" she called. "Mark here is coming up." She waved me on. "Allen'll be up there poring over all of them looking for the ugliest."

∽

Allen sat in a small bedroom at the end of the upstairs hall. He was sitting cross legged. The lights were off, but a little daylight penetrated a thin curtain. A suitcase lay open in front of him.

"You don't need to give us any of those," I said. "I mean, if you're planning to sell them or whatever."

"I don't want them." He kicked the suitcase my way, a quick, violent movement. "Don't even like them anymore. They just sit here."

"Maybe give them to—"

"—Just take a bunch."

I stepped into the room. The place smelled of mold. A forked crack ran up the far wall. I crouched over the suitcase. It was piled every which way with ebony carvings—bald heads, sharp faces, empty eyes, and bare breasts, a whole army of them, some almost a foot tall.

I rose without taking one. "Sheri and I should probably be off. We're going to the hospital—"

"—I don't know why you brought the insulin back. Tim doesn't even hardly live here anymore."

"It was just the address on the container."

"He uses the place like a hotel. I told Mom to kick him out."

"Well," I said, but couldn't think of anything to add. I set my hand on the dresser and half turned towards the door, only it seemed rude to simply walk away.

Allen scooted forward a little and kicked the suitcase a second time. The carvings rattled. "My best friend over there was named Mark. Half these things are really his." He rubbed his nose with the heel of his hand. "He shot himself though so I guess it hardly matters." He sniffled a moment, and looked at me in silence.

I took a step back across the carpet. The sloped ceiling was just inches from my head.

"They'd eat you alive in Africa," he said. "With that thing in your mouth. And that hair."

I'd backed as far as the door, but those words stopped me.

"When I was on leave in Nairobi, I had two whores in my room both better looking than your girlfriend."

"She's my sister," I said, but Allen wasn't listening.

"Talk about stacked. Over here a girl like that wouldn't look at you twice. Over there I had two at once. My Sergeant had three in his room. He took pictures, too, but one of them stole his camera." Allen lifted a rifle from where it leaned against the wall then sat back down on the floor. "This is what he did. Mark Elliot. He put a pen through the trigger loop down here, opened his mouth, stepped down on the pen and boom." Allen set the rifle butt between his feet, held the barrel near the muzzle and opened his mouth. He tapped both feet on the floor as though he was going to push the trigger.

"Allen," Mrs Mundson called.

We both glanced towards the stairs. She called again.

"Ignore her. She'll shut up after a while. Pass me that pen on the desk."

"Come on down here, Allen."

It took him a moment to balance the pen on the trigger. He set his feet to hold it in place. It wasn't until he had it all set up and was returning the muzzle to his mouth that I said, "What are you doing?" My palms were damp and my heart clamoured.

"Had a Christmas Eve party. Mark was back in quarters, depressed and all. He was supposed to be calling his parents, but instead he went to his bunk, picked up his weapon and blew his head off."

Allen opened his mouth and set his teeth on the muzzle. His toes held the pen against the trigger. I reached out. I tried to tell him to stop, but my throat was dry. The word came out as a croak. My finger tips touched the barrel and Allen raised his head.

"Only you wouldn't do it with a twenty-two."

The stairs creaked. We both turned our heads, and the rifle fell to the floor.

"Hello?" It was Sheri. "Hello up there?"

"Just a sec," I said. "We'll be right down."

"Blood was all over. We tried to clean it up, but it was dark."

In the hallway each tread creaked. Sheri was moving slowly. The staircase wasn't lit and she'd be feeling her way.

"Christmas morning some of his brains were still in the wall's cracks. They say it was the malaria drugs. Makes you depressed and all."

"Hi." Sheri stood in the doorway. She stepped forward, touched my shoulder. "We should go."

Allen stood. "Hold on a minute." He collected an armful of carvings, unloaded them on Sheri.

She protested, she said we couldn't.

"I don't want them anymore. You too," Allen said. "Come here."

Sheri tried to return some, but Allen wouldn't let her near the suitcase. One slipped from her grip and hit the floor.

Allen laid a dozen of them in my arms and my body suddenly began to quiver. As I took hold of the carvings, a ripple of relief ran from my chest to my fingers.

"Allen, honestly," Sheri said.

"Give them away. I don't give a fuck. I'm going to burn the rest like fucking firewood." He pushed the suitcase into the corner and closed its lid.

"But we don't need all these," Sheri said. "How about one? I'll take one."

"Just take them," I snapped then I turned to Allen. "Thank you."

Downstairs Mrs. Mundson asked Allen why he was giving us so many. "How are you going to open up a store if you keep giving them away?"

"Shut up, Mom. I'm not opening a store, okay? I never even said I was opening a store."

She took in a sharp breath and shook her head. "I don't know what's gotten into you, I swear."

"Could you just shut up a second?"

Allen led us to the porch and Mrs Mundson followed. Sheri promised if we saw Tim, we'd bring him home.

"You do that," Mrs Mundson said from the doorway.

"He won't come with you. He practically lives over at the Hendersons now."

Mrs Mundson said to hush.

Beyond the field the sun was preparing a beautiful exit—a bright red ball hanging above the horizon, spreading its colours into wispy clouds.

We set our carvings in the back of the car. Sheri took the driver's seat and revved the engine.

As we pulled away, Mrs Mundson waved. Allen stuck his hands deep in his pockets, turned and headed in.

At the end of the block, Sheri said, "Wasn't that bizarre? I mean, my God." She shook her head, raised a hand and looked at me. "So what were you two doing up there?"

I told her Allen had been talking about Rwanda.

"Oh," Sherri said.

I didn't mention the rifle. Nor did I tell her that the boy we'd given a ride wasn't Tim Mundson.

After that, neither of us said much at all, not on the ride to Kingston and not in the hospital either. Sheri even forgot to bring in the Bible.

We sat quietly with Grandfather and then we had dinner in the cafeteria. Afterwards we took the elevator up for a final goodbye. Sheri held Grandfather's hand a moment, bent over and kissed him. She whispered something. When she backed away, I did the same. I leaned close enough that our cheeks touched. I whispered goodbye and good luck and gave him a kiss. I don't know why I said good luck. It just came out like that.

Back at the car, Sheri collected an armful of Allen's carvings. She carried them across the parking lot to a dumpster and returned for another load. "I can't have these around," she said. "They're creepy. I didn't want them from the beginning."

80

"Allen wouldn't care. He just wanted to get rid of them."

When Sheri wasn't looking, I pocketed one of the smaller carvings. It was a woman's face with high cheeks, a sharp nose and a hint of a smile.

Sheri returned to the car and climbed into the back seat. She searched it thoroughly, even felt along the floor to make sure she'd gotten every last one.

As my sister guided us out of the lot and drove north towards the highway, I dug my hand into my coat pocket, ran it over the smooth surface of the wood and gave the little figure a squeeze. Something I'd been waiting for had happened tonight. It was like a whip cracked so close to my back I could feel it.

We splashed through puddles on the empty streets. The tarmac glistened. As we neared the 401, the moon emerged from clouds and winked at us. Inside and outside, all was silent.

LUCKY STREAK

After I lost my job, my wife hung up her shingle as a massage therapist. She emailed friends and family, told co-workers from her day job, put an ad on Craigslist and bought a secondhand massage table. When it wasn't in use, we folded the table in half, turned it on its side and set the TV on top of it.

The first night we had the table, the Giants were at the end of a three game home stand against the Dodgers. They were behind a few runs, and by the seventh inning I was channel surfing and came across a woman massaging a man's back. "Look at this," I said to Marti, but she had her eyes closed. On TV, the man rolled over. He had a hard-on poking up against the sheet.

"I'll take care of that," the woman said, and as the camera closed in on her face, she gave him a hand job.

I nudged Marti. "You missed it."

Marti sat up and rubbed her eyes.

"Any of the men you massaged ever get hard ons?"

"Get what?"

"Back when you used to work at the spa, did your customers ever get horny during the massage?"

"David, what are you talking about?"

"Never mind. Go back to sleep." I tossed a pillow her way. It landed in her lap. She picked it up and threw it back.

Sophie started crying just then and Marti stood. "Coming."

She stretched and yawned. "For the record, it was a women's day spa."

"Oh," I said. "They ever get turned on?"

"David, the things you don't know could fill a book."

"Giants are getting their asses kicked again," I said, but she'd already closed the door.

This is the story of Marti and me three years ago, the story of our lives together, our family back when Sophie was a toddler, when we lived in the ground floor apartment of a run down Victorian in the Mission. Marti was working full time as a legal secretary, but she wanted to get back into massage, wanted to do something with her hands, wanted to be her own boss and choose her own hours. I was trying to get on unemployment, trying to take care of Sophie, and I did some of the work setting up Marti's massage business.

This is also the story of what happened when Jason Everett walked into our lives. He was Marti's first client and became her only regular. One morning he emailed her complaining of back problems and they set up an appointment for that evening. Marti and I temporarily converted the living room into a massage studio—candles, scented oils and New Age music. We turned the space heater on half-an-hour before the appointment and covered the furniture with a few hand-batiked scarves from Marti's hippie-dippie days. I waited outside with Sophie, walked her up the block past a couple of kids in a truck blaring salsa music. We turned around at the corner where the trash can is always overflowing. "Some boys wear underwear," she said as we passed the guys in the truck for the second time. Sophie was two and a half, and she'd started to say the funniest things.

At five after eight, a lanky man in an overcoat knocked on our door. I stood across the street watching the apartment window until Marti closed the curtains. That was the signal all was well. Sophie and I headed for Dolores Park.

Since losing my job, I'd taken Sophie to the park once or twice a day—an easy way to kill an hour, and for a long time, I didn't know what else to do with her. She loved the swing. She hung out the front of the baby seat, demanded that I push her on every pass. She liked the slide too, the curly one that had been tagged so often it was a work of art. On this particular evening, there were enough kids that she couldn't stay on the swing long. When I took her out, she ran off to the slide. There was a Frisbee in the sand by the ladder and I showed her how it worked, wrapped her little fingers around it then ran a few steps forward so she could throw it to me.

"Ready?" she said. It sailed off towards the swing. "You catch," she said.

"Okay. This time I will."

I jogged over and picked it up. On her second attempt, she held it upside down. I didn't correct her. It flew closer to me, but still way out of reach. "Holy moly." She ran after it herself this time.

She threw it again—without any attempt to head it in my direction then slowly worked her way around the sandy area, throwing and chasing, and managing not to hit any other kids. Eventually, she threw it too far onto the grass and a Great Dane ran off with it.

"Frisbee!" Sophie screamed.

I ran after the dog, up towards the trench where the street car runs and the drug dealers work. Sophie ran after me. Eventually, the Great Dane's owner caught the dog, held the metal studded collar and negotiated with him. Finally he threw the disc back.

The Great Dane barked and strained his owners grip. "Home time," I said and we took the long way back to kill a few extra minutes.

Marti was standing at our front door talking with the man in the overcoat. I slowed to try and give him time to leave. Marti laughed, flashed her teeth, tilted her head, and just then Sophie spotted her. "I see Mama." She leaned forward in the stroller. She strained against the straps. Marti looked at us and waved as I walked up.

"David, meet Jason. Jason, this is my husband and my daughter."

He bent a little. "Well, howdy doody." Sophie turned and pressed her face against the side of the stroller. Jason straightened. "Lucky man, you," he said. "Wife with hands like that." He had a wide, thick forehead above sunken eyes—bright little opals set in recessed sockets. I had a hard time not staring at those eyes.

"David doesn't like massages," Marti said.

"Not true. Just needs to be the right moment."

"I like them at the right moment too," Jason said. "It's just that the right moment always happens to be now."

Marti bent and unbuckled Sophie. "Come give me a hug and tell me that you love me."

Just to get it out up front, my boss fired me for gross negligence. One day I got to work and didn't feel like processing orders, so I just stopped. For almost three weeks, I sat at my desk, took long walks, played on the computer, hung out in the lunch room. And then she fired me.

This wasn't the first time I'd been unemployed. I'd had that rush of guilt and the slow steady build of money panic before, but this time felt different. We were a family. I had Sophie to take care of, and I took on the wifely duties. While Marti earned the dough, I cooked and cleaned.

After Jason's first massage, Marti put Sophie to sleep and I cleaned up. I dumped the sheets in the hamper, folded the table, put it in the corner and set the TV back on top. When I was finished, I collected two beers, put up my feet and switched on the baseball game.

Dusty Baker was piloting the Giants through some teething pains as spring turned to summer that year. The team had the makings of a pennant winner though—structure, talent, depth in pitching staff, good hitters, and this night, for the first time in weeks, they were shining. Up half a dozen runs on the Marlins.

Marti eased the bedroom door shut and tiptoed my way. "That guy needs a few massages," she said. "He was about as ropey as they come."

We clinked beer bottles, and I put the TV on mute.

"He had these big strange tattoos along his back," she said.

"That's a swift move. Tattoos on your back."

"Got them while he was in the Navy. On liberty in Manila for twenty-four hours and got so drunk he passed out. His buddies got the tattoos done. He was telling me this as you two walked up. They told him he'd gotten in a fight and someone smashed up his back. It was two weeks before he figured out what really happened."

The TV cut to a shot of the dugout, caught Barry Bonds' scowl.

"You got a winner there," I said.

"He was actually kind of funny. Nice guy."

JT Snow knocked one out of the park just then, right out into the Bay where fans had gathered in boats hoping to catch a ball. The TV camera caught the splash—a little blip of white spray between a yacht and a dinghy.

"So?" Marti said.

I raised my bottle. "Thank you for the sixty bucks, Jason."

Marti touched her beer against mine.

"He get a hard on?" I asked.

"David."

"Just wondering. We saw it on TV, remember. It's natural."

"Of course he didn't. It's a therapeutic massage. Plus I worked on his back the whole time."

"Good. That means he can come again."

"Very funny," she said and set her beer on the end table.

We both watched the silent TV. I was about to take off the mute when she said, "You apply to any jobs today?"

"Sophie didn't nap until late and then I had to get dinner started."

"Ever think maybe you should learn about computers? That guy Jason was saying—"

"—I already know about computers."

"I mean really know them. More than how to turn one on."

"Can't teach an old dog new tricks."

"Say things like that and you'll never get a job."

Marti leaned over, rested her head on the sofa's arm and watched the TV in silence. I took it off mute.

Later that week I took Sophie to visit Marti at work. We walked all the way to Van Ness station, partially to kill time, partially to share in the bustle of life on Mission. The taqueria on 20th vents its grill onto the street and coats the corner in the smell of roasting meat; next door a store sells Coke and Pepsi imported from Mexico; beyond that a pair of tiendas have their windows plastered with calling card flyers. Tere's Beauty Salon is two doors up from Tere's II, and the rest of the block is produce stands and a narrow store displaying sequined high heels for little girls. Strains of music float along the street—Merengue, Marimba or whatever—big brass sounds, crooning vocals, a chorus of guitars.

At this end of Mission the palms are tall, Dr. Seuss-like trees—little heads of foliage on long pipe-cleaner necks. They swayed above us as we walked past a few men standing aimlessly, a woman selling Michoacan Helados from a cart, old men slapping dominos on a makeshift table. The shoeshine man smiled at us, showed the gold stars implanted in his eye teeth.

After we got on MUNI, Sophie started singing, "Daddy likes to go poo-poo and pee-pee." I gave her a licorice to keep her quiet.

The receptionist knows us. She buzzed Marti as soon as we stepped off the elevator. Sophie played with the two little ferns while I looked at the certificates and awards posted on the walls. I've read each about a thousand times, but I do it whenever we wait for Marti. "Tops at the Three T's of Teamwork." Four years in a row of "The Safety First Award". "San Francisco AIDS walk 1999."

Marti walked around the corner, spread her arms, crouched and hugged Sophie.

"Daddy likes to go poo-poo and pee-pee," Sophie said.

Marti looked up at me then stood.

"She's been saying that all morning. I don't know where she gets this stuff."

"I'm in a meeting. You should have called."

I nodded and gave a bit of a grimace. Marti was always in meetings.

Sophie and I headed back to Marti's cubicle. I sat there with Sophie on my lap listening to the undulating conversations around us while Sophie banged on the keyboard and searched through Marti's pens, pencils, post-its and paperclips. She's only allowed to go through Marti's top drawer. The drawers below are all off limits.

The woman in the cubicle across from Marti's held out a Hershey Kiss. She mouthed "May I?" to me, but Sophie was already over there. She walked back holding it up like a trophy.

Finally Marti returned, both hands smoothing down her pleated wool skirt. "All right. Lets do the rounds."

She led Sophie down the hall then leaned her head back in to speak to me. "You have to find something else to do with her. You can't come here all the time, okay?"

"I thought you liked it."

"I know. I just. I don't know."

"We haven't come in a week."

"Fine. Forget it. I just figured the library, the rec-centre, the zoo."

I leaned way back in Marti's chair and closed my eyes. All around me people typed, nattered on the phone, shuffled papers, did the things that folks in offices do. When companies as big as this one lay off a thousand people, I've often wondered how they function the next day. What did all those people do? How can a thousand people just drop their jobs?

The woman in the nearby cubicle slid her seat forward. "Is your name David?"

I swivelled to face her. Her hair was pulled back in a bun and it made her face look perfectly round. I nodded, and tried to smile.

"Alice," she said. She sipped from her water bottle.

I pointed at Marti's computer. "I'd log in but no password. You have one I could use?"

She shook her head, edged her chair back to her desk and returned to work.

After about ten minutes, Marti came back. "Tour over. Time to get back to work."

Sophie held up a pair of pens. "Okay. Back to work."

"No, that means I work, you go play."

Sophie gave me one of her pens to look over. "Fantastic," I said. She got the same company pens every time we came. *Motivated. Empowered. Accountable.*

Sophie climbed back into the stroller. As I pushed her out, she said, "I have invisible friend?"

Among other things, this story is also about how a child can change a life.

As summer crept up on us that year, Jason became a regular. There were other customers—a bicycle messenger whose insurance settlement provided five free massages, a woman who insisted lymph drainage had cured her cancer, a mother and daughter who lined up massages as a break during their Shopping-in-the-City weekend. But Jason was Marti's regular, her only weekly client.

One evening in June, Jason's massage went late. Sophie was asleep in the stroller, so it wasn't a bother. I sat on Leroy's steps, rocked the stroller and waited, ball game crackling on my transistor radio, and after ten or fifteen minutes our door opened.

Jason didn't step out, so I stood, leaned forward and glanced inside. Darkness. I pushed Sophie over the threshold. Jason was still there, leaning against the massage table. Marti was sitting on the sofa opposite him.

"Just running your wife into over time," Jason said.

"You'll never believe this," Marti said. "His daughter was abducted."

"Not quite abducted. It's a long story. Didn't mean to keep you waiting out there."

"He got his girlfriend pregnant then ran off to join the navy."

Jason held up both hands. "It sounds worse than it was. Her mother and me were kids when she got pregnant. I joined the Navy, she hooked up with this other guy, Fred Appleby—married him, and put his name on the birth certificate as the father. Anyway, I was just telling your wife this whole story. Three years later, I pulled in here on liberty. I'd had zero contact since leaving. I didn't even know if the kid was a boy or a girl, and she was two by this point, just as cute as this little one here. Broke my heart and changed my life." He paused and licked his lips.

"Wow," I said.

"No," Marti said. "That's not it. That's not the whole story."

"All right. Making a long story short here, my ex wasn't about to go back on saying Fred was the father, so I played along as the uncle. A few months later, I wrangled a posting here, back when they had a base at Alameda. I took her once a week. Best three years of my life, although I didn't realize it then. I thought it would go on forever. When Saddam invaded Kuwait, I got posted over there—one of the first over. Boom, I'm gone." He clapped.

"Are you listening?" Marti said.

"Course I'm listening. Just trying to keep Sophie from slumping over so bad."

"While I'm gone, my ex was killed by a drunk driver, and when I got back Fred had disappeared with my daughter."

"See the problem is," Marti said. "She's Fred's kid in all the paperwork. Everyone thinks he's the dad, so it's not legally an abduction."

"I took a leave of absence, spent two years and all my savings looking for her. Hired a private investigator. It's been twelve years since I saw her. I never stopped looking. I never stopped hoping. Today's her birthday. She turned eighteen. Only I don't even know what State she's in."

"Well, maybe she'll find you."

"Maybe," he said and looked straight at me with those sunken eyes. "You never know."

After Jason left, Marti took Sophie into the bedroom and I returned the room to normal. I perched the TV on the folded massage table

91

and moved the CD rack off the filing cabinet. With five years worth of junk, the apartment always felt crowded, even with everything in its place.

Marti came out just as I was settling on the sofa. "Can't sleep?" I said.

She shook her head. "Been thinking about Jason and his daughter. That story."

"Yeah." I put my feet on the coffee table. "Ever think it's odd a guy pays sixty bucks every week for a rub down?"

"How do you mean odd?"

"I don't know, just—"

"—Lots of people charge more."

"I know it's worth it. I just. I figure a guy's got one thing on his mind."

"The man tells a heart-wrenching story about losing his daughter and this is what you're thinking?"

"I'm thinking he sure wants your sympathy."

"For Christ sakes, David, he's here for medical reasons. He's got a bad back. He sits at a desk all day. I keep him going."

"You know what you can get for sixty bucks at 16th and Mission."

"It's sixty bucks that keeps him from the unemployment line, which is more than I can say for some."

"Oh, okay. We're back to that, are we?"

"No, we're not back to that."

Marti looked up at the ceiling and her Adams apple bobbed, a faint movement on the surface of pale skin. Without looking back at me, she said, "You do have to get out of this rut though."

"I sent out a couple of resumés today. Bought some nice paper so they look good."

"David, what world do you live in? People don't print their resumés any more."

"It looks professional. Appearance counts. They get emailed stuff every day. I'm just another forty-year-old with a string of jobs. This, they're really going to notice. Believe me."

"Look," she said, but she didn't finish that sentence. "David, do you think you ever really wanted something? Really really. I mean like Jason devoting his life to finding his kid. Do you think you've ever wanted something so bad?"

"Don't know. Never thought about it."

"That's your problem," Marti said. "You don't have a fire burning. You never really want anything."

"I used to want things. Maybe it's age. Maybe I'm turning into a blob."

"You know what I want? I want a normal life."

"I will get a job, Marti. Eventually."

"I don't just mean that. I'm tired of this. Of living here. Of working all day and half my nights—"

"—For the record, I haven't found it particularly easy to take care of Sophie—"

"—That's not what I'm saying. There are homeless people sleeping on our street, David. There's glass and needles at the park and gang bangers cruising the neighborhood. Wouldn't it be nice to own a house, raise Sophie with a backyard, somewhere to play that isn't two blocks from hookers and drug dealers?"

"I've told you a million times, I won't live in the suburbs."

"Oh, for Christ sakes, David. There's lots of nice towns nearby. You're looking for a job. Maybe now's the time. Send out some applications to Eureka, Chico, Sebastopol. Places like that."

"I don't know."

"Lisa told me she'd keep an eye on jobs for you in Eureka. At the college and all. No harm trying."

"I guess," I said, and ran my hand across the two day stubble of my cheek. A conversation like this is best ended by just shutting up, so I switched on the TV.

That night in bed, I listened to Sophie asleep in the cot, her breath the faintest of whispers, and for an instant there in the darkness, I knew I could be as determined as Jason and follow this tiny body to the corners of the earth.

If there was a moment that summer that I understood how lucky I was, this was it. I set a hand on her back and left it there, sensing the rise and fall of her chest and the beating of her heart.

Summer brought the fog. It blew in from the headlands, crept up from Ocean Beach and through Richmond. It blanketed the city that year, hung low every afternoon, thick enough by nightfall that you could open your mouth and taste it.

The summer was cold, but we had the hottest baseball since 1989. The Giants posted a 32 and 23 record in July and August and put a playoff berth within reach. Bonds was hitting his stride, chasing the home run title, and they traded for Kenny Lofton, a veteran fielder with speed and a strong left-handed swing.

The fog may have fuelled the Giants, but it also emptied the city every weekend. People streamed up and down the coast and into the mountains for a taste of summer heat and sun. Marti made regular trips to Eureka to see her sister. Mostly I preferred the city, although once that summer I did join them.

Lisa had moved to Eureka three years before. She's got no kids, and no man in her life, but moving there meant she could afford a house—a little place on a deep lot that backs onto a ravine. It was after Lisa moved that Marti started bugging me about getting out of the city.

Marti honked as we pulled in and Lisa came out, flower print dress billowing around her. She crouched and gave Sophie a hug, then hugged her sister then turned to me and said, "Brother-in-law." I let her hug me too.

Lisa and Marti worked on dinner, while I read Sophie *The Cat in the Hat*. Afterwards, I opened a beer and sat at the kitchen table with my transistor radio. Lisa doesn't have a TV. That's okay by me. Baseball's a game of words, numbers, and stats—a thinking man's game, a sport well summed up in language. While Lisa and Marti nattered away, I let my mind drift into the broadcast, into Jon Miller's sharp voice and his choppy play-by-play.

"Hey, David, we're ready to serve. Will you turn that thing off?"

I opened my eyes, looked over at Lisa, wine glass in her hand. It was top of the sixth in a two run game, but I switched it off.

"It's his security blanket," Marti said. "It keeps him from having to interact with other people. Isn't that right, David?"

I pushed the radio from me. "Well, all right, what fascinating subjects are you discussing?"

"Bonds' batting average," Lisa said, and Marti stifled a laugh.

"Which is?"

They looked at each other. Marti gulped from her wine. "Fifty?" Lisa said.

"You two have had too much to drink already."

"How about this one, David: what would you call batting average for a job seeker? Resumé average?"

I switched the radio back on.

"Oh, come on, I'm just joking. We're nearly ready to eat. Help set the table." Marti put her glass on the counter. "David here's become a superstar housekeeper."

Sophie sat on a pair of phone books so she could reach her plate. She ate quickly—mashed potatoes and chicken strips, finished everything but the green beans, then pulled on Marti's hand. "Story time," she said.

"Give me a second, Sweetie. I'm still eating."

I stood. "I'll do it."

"No," Sophie said. "I want Mama. Special Mama time." I sat back down. Marti took a couple more bites then headed for the living room. Even before I started staying home with her, Sophie never asked for special Dada time.

Lisa refilled my wine glass.

"I take it the job search isn't going so well?"

"Do we have to talk about that?"

"No. We could talk about Bonds' batting average again."

"Or we could talk about nothing."

"You know depression is treatable, David. You could see someone. I've told Marti this half a dozen times."

"It's not depression. I'm just in a rut."

"There's nothing to be ashamed of. Lots of times it's a simple chemical imbalance they can fix."

"I wouldn't ever take meds. My mother took meds."

"It's different now, David."

A bird arrived at the feeder just beyond the window. It twittered, flapped its wings and was off. Another landed on the feeder's roof. "Strange to hear more birds than sirens," I said.

Lisa didn't say anything for a while. A smaller bird circled the feeder. "The reverse of that is an extremely disturbing thought, David."

"More sirens than birds? Just happens when you've got more people around. Live in the wilderness and you'll never hear a siren, guaranteed."

"Think of Sophie's perspective, though. Isn't more sirens than birds a disturbing environment for a kid?"

"You can raise a kid in the city, Lisa. Millions of kids are leading perfectly good lives in downtowns all over the country."

"Don't know that Marti feels that way."

"Are you now Marti's agent or counsel or something?" I tried to smile but no doubt it came off forced, like so much between Lisa and me.

She stood. "Might go read Sophie a story myself," she said.

I switched the transistor back on and sat there among the dirty dishes. It wasn't my house. These weren't my dishes. Outside the birds twittered. On the radio Jon Miller gave the count.

I'd grown up in the mess of southern California just after Major League ball arrived there, and while the term urban sprawl was being defined: house after house, street after street, development after development, a growing uniformed army standing at attention miles from anywhere. Not for me. No thanks.

Before Sophie's bedtime, in the long, angular shadows of a summer evening, the two of us walked to the ravine behind Lisa's house—a tangle of mossy ferns and underbrush. A tall stand of redwoods casts darkness down across the slope.

96

Sophie crossed into the forest as though testing herself, stepped into the shadow without holding my hand. She glanced back, ran a few steps ahead of me then stopped and turned. "I want hold you," she said and ran back.

I carried her for a little, then she asked to go back inside.

"The forest," she said. "It's not broken, right?"

"No, I guess it's not."

The next week, Jason was back for another massage, and the week after. He came at least once a week through the final days of summer, while the Giants fought for a playoff berth and Bonds racked up homer after homer. Labor Day weekend I sent off a couple of resumés, went to a ball game, and Marti visited her sister again. They looked at real estate. It was important to her, and what was I supposed to say? She was just looking.

Monday night, she was back with a folder full of listings. One was near Lisa's: a bungalow, stucco and grey. Nothing special. I held the sheet close trying to make out the fine print.

"Show me the bank that's going to lend three hundred thousand dollars to an unemployed forty-year-old and his wife," I said.

"Just forget it." She grabbed at the folder, but I pulled it away, tucked it behind my back.

"The place looks nice. Very nice. Just let me finish looking at the pictures."

Marti left. I flipped through the others, then set the folder on top of the refrigerator so life could roll on.

One evening that September, I brought Sophie back early. Marti was still working on Jason and I almost walked in on them. As I stood with my hand on the door knob, muted voices reached me, and the plucking of guitar strings on the stereo. Jason laughed, then Marti said something.

"Dada," Sophie called. "Dada, I want hold you."

I left the stroller on the walkway and tried to peek through the living room windows, but the blinds were pulled. I waved back at

Sophie to entertain her while I held my ear to the glass. A car cruised past, super base thump-thumping and then the door opened. I had time to step away from the window, then Jason was outside. He glanced my way, ran a hand across his mouth. He stepped around Sophie's stroller. "What's up?" he said.

"Just cleaning up the flowers. Had a few minutes to kill." I plucked a dead head off a gladiola in the window box.

Jason looked at his watch and started walking.

While Marti put Sophie to bed, I cleaned up. Jason's sheets were spread tight across the table. The top sheet lay precisely enough that I couldn't be sure a body had ever been between the sheets. As I crouched in front of the table, my mind danced over all sorts of configurations and possibilities. When Marti finally opened the bedroom door, I tore the sheets off and dumped them in the hamper.

All that following week, change hung in the air. September warmed the city and burned off summer's fog. Marti had given up trying to get new massage clients. Life with a child was getting easier. Sophie was almost three. I'd found some sort of rhythm to the process of sending out resumés. In all these things and more, I could feel a shift ahead.

The evening of Jason's next appointment, I came back early again. This time I walked right in. The room was dim and hot. A piano was tinkling away on the stereo. Jason wasn't even on the table. He was standing, leaning against it, arms folded, buck naked, all of him hanging out for the world to see. He'd been saying something when I barged in. He checked himself then turned to face me. Marti was on the sofa.

"Well, what the fuck," I managed to say.

"Jesus Christ, David, will you just give us a second here?"

"Mama," Sophie called from outside. "Mama."

"Please," Marti said.

I stepped back out, fidgeted in front of the house, then sat on Leroy's steps, my heart still thundering, an ache spreading out from my breastbone. Three months I'd been walking Sophie around with my head in the clouds. Three months. What the fuck was he doing in there swinging his cock about in my livingroom?

When my breath had slowed and evened, I lifted Sophie from the stroller.

"I see Mama," she said. She pushed at me, struggled in my arms. "I see Mama now."

Behind me our door opened then clicked closed.

I set Sophie back in the stroller and buckled the straps while she flailed about. I had her in before Jason passed me on the sidewalk. He raised a hand and looked my way without speaking.

"Now hold on a second," I said.

Jason stopped and turned. He squinted at me and cocked his head. "I was just getting dressed," he said.

I took a step closer, but then our door opened again. "David," Marti called and Jason moved on.

My hands squeezed the bar of the stroller. My knuckles blanched, and I pushed Sophie inside. "So he's here for back problems?" I said.

Marti bent. She took Sophie out of the stroller.

"Before you begin your rant, just let me get Sophie to bed."

"Absolutely. Be my guest."

"Pyjama time," she said.

"I figured there had to be a reason he kept coming back when no one else did."

"Oh shut up, David." She slammed the bedroom door. I cleaned up a little, got the living room somewhat normal, and in a few minutes, Marti had Sophie down. She pulled the door shut behind herself, latched it gently.

"Look, I'm the one who has to deal with it, not you," she said.

"I just never expected to see my wife gabbing with a naked guy in my own house."

"So he likes to be naked, big deal."

"Well it's over. He's not coming back." My hand sliced the air between us, a short chopping motion.

"Right?" I said, and while I waited for her answer, my eyes shifted focus, and I caught my own reflection in the window: a figure worn away by years of just trying to get by.

"He's practically my only client," she said at last. "And he does pay more of the rent than you."

"Oh, lovely. I see."

"Jesus, David, you're always looking for another reason to feel sorry for yourself. Poor you, you got fired. Poor you, you're forty. Poor you, your wife saw someone else's penis. I don't know if you need meds or counselling or what, but you need something."

"There's a principle involved here," I said. Marti shook her head and started walking down the hall towards the kitchen. "Don't you see?"

"If you don't want him back, get a God-damned job."

After a few days of thinking about it, I figured I'd seen the last of Jason. Who would return after an encounter like that? The morning of what would have been his next appointment, I suggested we put Sophie down early, cook a special meal, have a date night.

"Jason's coming tonight," Marti said. She finished her coffee and stood.

"You sure? I figured after what happened last week."

"I haven't heard otherwise."

Marti kissed Sophie goodbye and didn't say anything else.

My mind's synapses rapid-fired all day. When you spend that much time with an almost-three year old, the brain ticks through too many thoughts. How could she be so sure? And what would it mean if he did come back? One thing was obvious in all scenarios I could conceive: he was fulfilling some perverted desire, and no one involved cared if I knew or didn't. Just how is a man supposed to deal with that?

I took Sophie for a walk that evening, mostly because I thought Marti was wrong, but after a quick coffee stop at The Bagelry, we returned and the blinds were pulled. I tried to peek in the window but couldn't make out anything. The tinkle of piano keys was the only sound.

"Hello," I called, but not very loudly. "We're out here," I said.

Behind me, Sophie shouted. I walked past her, hands worrying each other, my breath short and loud. I paced the sidewalk as though I needed some momentum, then turned, headed for the door.

Just then, Marti stepped out. "What the hell is going on?"

"I just." I held up my hands. "Sophie's sick," I said. "Listen to her." By this point she was wailing.

Marti leaned back inside and said, "Give me a second." She walked out to Sophie, put a hand on the girl's forehead. Sophie reached for her, stretched against the stroller's straps. "Mama, I want hold you."

I took Marti's hand as she leaned over Sophie. I pulled her away, put an arm around her.

"David." She pushed at me.

"What?"

"Let go."

"Lets dance."

"Have you like, completely lost it?"

"Marti."

"Just go walk her around the God damned block and give me a second. It's time to pull yourself together."

Marti and I were only together another year, but when it ended, it wasn't because of Jason or anyone like him. She moved up to Eureka to stay with her sister and took Sophie. Now I see her school holidays and every second weekend. I'm still in the city, still in that same apartment.

Nights in the summer, while fog curls around the windows, closes in and cuts me off, I think of that summer before Sophie turned three, those months when I had her to myself, and I think of Jason and his daughter. I don't know what happened to him, whether he found her, whether the story was even true, but what I think, when I think of Jason, is that I should be up in Eureka, following wherever Sophie goes, hoping for another lucky break instead of letting my chance drift by.

That last night Jason came, I didn't say anything to Marti, and she didn't raise the topic with me. The answering machine was blinking and the message was a job offer from a manager I'd worked for years ago. They needed someone to tag and track clothing in a little garment factory in the outer Mission. That message carried us away. We opened beers and watched some TV. I told her this was it: our lives were changing, looking up again.

"I just needed a chance like this, something to get me back on my feet."

"I hope so."

I raised my glass. "Better days are coming. Things are looking up."

Sophie was in the cot when we got into bed. As we settled in, Marti shifted over, pulled herself close and kissed me. She put an arm around me. I kissed back, ran a hand along her ribs and down her back and pressed us together. For a moment there in the darkness, I was sure she was smiling at me. When she rolled back, I slid on top of her.

That phone message was the start of a string of good luck. I started my new job the next week, Marti cancelled Jason's appointments, she sold her massage table, and we used the money to hire a babysitter and go to the first game of the playoffs—the Giants and the Braves. Our guys went on to win that series. They faced off for the National League title, rode that wave right up until Game Seven of the World Series.

Like all streaks of luck though, this one came to an end. Like all good things, it came to an end too early, before anyone had the chance to really appreciate it.

MARTIN AND LISA

Martin raised his glass, and with the rest of the crowd called, "Happy Retirement." While most of the glasses were still in the air someone shouted, "Lets see it now, Carl. Come on."

Those who knew what this meant clapped and called out, and Martin's father set down the microphone and held up a hand as though reluctantly submitting. He folded his arms, squatted and kicked out his legs like a young Cossack. People clapped and cheered, then on Carl's fourth or fifth kick, his foot slipped. He lost his balance and landed on his back. For a moment, he lay still.

The clapping stopped and everything went quiet. When Martin stepped forward, his father shifted and sat up. "Give me a God-damned hand here."

Martin crouched and helped him up.

The moment Carl stood, the guests returned to cheering and clapping. Carl waved and took a bow.

"All right, show's over, back to your drinks." He dug a finger into his collar and pulled at it.

At the other end of the marquee, someone called, "I'll file the law suit for you Monday morning."

"You going to be okay?" Martin asked, but his father had already turned his back and was bending one knee as though testing it.

"Fucking floor tiles laid wrong." Carl started walking. Martin followed. After a few paces, Lisa caught up and tucked her arm into Martin's.

When they reached the makeshift bar, Carl turned to face them. His trademark big-toothed grin was back. "I've got a joke for you. Lisa, you'll be able to relate. What do the wives of alcoholics and law grads have in common?" Carl poured himself a scotch. The corner of his mouth twitched. "Both are Bar widows."

"Oh, that's funny," Lisa said.

Martin gave a brief chuckle.

Carl pointed his drink Martin's way. "Lisa, he ever tell you that when I was his age, I was first in my class and first at the Bar too?"

"Of course he did," Lisa said.

"No he didn't. You're just being polite." Carl still had his drink held out towards Martin. "You cut a good one out of the herd here, Son."

Martin picked up the nearest bottle of wine and poured two glasses. "You could make the same joke about retiring lawyers and alcoholics. 'At the Bar too long.'"

When Martin looked up, his father had turned and was walking back towards the marquee where Martin's mother stood with the wives of Carl's former law partners. As he walked away, Carl cast a hand over his head and waved. "Today is the last day anyone will fear the mighty legal mind of Carleton Archer."

The music had started. Under the marquee, people were clearing away chairs to make space on the floor.

Martin took a long drink of wine. "What Dad means is that I should have been first in my class and had better be first at the Bar."

"'Cut a good one out of the herd'?" Lisa said. She squeezed herself, and her shoulders rose a little.

From beside the house, Martin's sister Carol waved. Lisa put her arm through Martin's again. "The torches along the laneway are all going out," she said. "Shall we go relight them?"

She pulled on Martin's arm, but he didn't move. Carol had started shuffling towards them. She held her hands up as if asking Martin and Lisa to hold still. "I've lost my drink and my husband, both in the past five minutes, and I can't decide which I'd rather have back." She pushed her tongue into her cheek and rolled her eyes. "Dad's in top form tonight."

"Did you notice his crooked bowtie?" Martin said. "It's been that way so long I don't think I can say anything."

"And you?" Carol reached out, brushed fingertips along Lisa's shoulder. "Still trying to live life through your Chakra? Am I saying that right? Chakra?"

Lisa smiled and shrugged at the same time.

"You're refreshing, Lisa. I'm always telling people it's great to have someone so fresh in the family."

"Thank you."

"And check out this dress. The polka dot look. My little Johnny likes polka dots too. You share a taste in clothes."

"This is Carol trying to be funny," Martin said.

"What's wrong with polka dots?" Lisa touched the front of her dress. She pinched it and edged a little closer to Martin.

"I'm always trying to be funny. Scott's smart and I'm funny. We're a good team. Scott's rich, I'm pretty. Or I was before Thing One and Thing Two. Pregnancy really does it to you, Lisa. Don't ever get that little body of yours pregnant."

"Carol," Martin said.

"I'll analyze you two. Okay, Martin, you're smart, Lisa you're, um..."

Lisa squeezed Martin's arm. "We should light the torches."

"Lisa, you're thin." Carol tilted her head. "You are quite thin. And Martin, you're kind hearted." She paused. "Lisa, I've got to think of another one for you."

"We should fix the torches before anyone thinks of leaving," Lisa said.

Martin took a step towards the lane. "If we see Scott, we'll let him know you're looking for him."

"Forget it. Changed my mind." She raised her right hand with a flourish. "I'd rather find my drink."

∼

Martin added fuel to the first torch, lit it, then continued down the lane towards the apple orchard. Lisa followed.

"You know, I was afraid of what she was going to say about me," Lisa said. "In her analysis thing. She's always a little mean to me."

"She just thinks she's being funny." Martin held his lighter to the torch's soft bristles and watched them catch.

"She's mean though, Martin. A lot of the time."

"She likes you," he said.

"She doesn't like me."

"What am I supposed to say, Lisa? She's my sister."

"I'm your wife."

"When Carol says something you don't like, just laugh and forget about it."

Martin crossed the lane, re-lit the next torch, then continued down the gravel drive. He expected Lisa to follow, but she didn't. For a while she just stood there at the top of the slope.

Where the lane met Bodega Bay Road, Martin turned to look back at the dim orange flames. Lisa was approaching between them. Martin dug the toe of his shoe into a small divot in the drive and dropped his gaze.

"It's like it would have been in the old days," she said. "A hundred years ago they'd have used torches like this to light everything."

Martin offered his hand, but Lisa didn't take it quickly enough and he let it drop. Strains of *Heartbreak Hotel* drifted up the lane. Martin turned towards the tent and began walking. After a moment, Lisa followed.

Carol and Carl were dancing at the edge of the crowd, moving in a rhythmic sway, their arms around each other and their bodies close.

Lisa cut two pieces of cake and offered one to Martin. He took it, then set it aside and picked up the glass he thought had been his.

"I ever tell you about the time I dropped Dad's birthday cake? Halfway through Happy Birthday, I let the plate tilt. Boom, there

106

it was on the floor—a couple of candles still burning. Dad pushed my face right up to it. Like you do when a dog craps in the house."

"That's awful."

"It was around the same time that he nicknamed me Pear. During my fat phase."

"I can't believe you were ever fat."

"Carol gathered up the cake, set it on the table all squished over and awful looking. Dad was still yelling at me, and Carol said 'If you don't come back to the table, neither of you gets any cake.' Mother used to defend him. It was Carol who was always on my side. Although somehow she wasn't against him either. Carol was sort of amazing."

Lisa opened her arms as though to envelop him, but Martin took her hand instead and led her towards the dance floor. They'd just begun to dance when the record skipped, hit a scratch then stopped all together. A few people groaned and almost everyone stopped dancing. Except for Carol and Carl. They swayed on in the corner by the stacked chairs.

Someone tried to find the right cut on the record. People called out. Carl took the cigar from his mouth. "I'll sing it for you. I'll sing it," he yelled, but just then the song started again at the beginning.

"Change partners?" Carol asked. She held out one hand for Martin. The other rested on her hip. Carl shrugged, returned the cigar to his mouth, and stepped towards Lisa, arms spread.

Lisa and Martin left just before two in the morning. Martin took back roads to the highway—narrow roads through forest so near the car that it felt like they were travelling at a great speed.

"The day Carol met Scott, I was the first person she told," Martin said. He kept his eyes on the road and both hands on the wheel. "I remember it so clearly. She'd only known him three hours, but she said, 'I'd marry him if he asked.' Can you believe that?"

Lisa didn't answer. She was already asleep in the passenger seat.

Martin slowed as he neared the on-ramp, passed through pools of light and onto the darkened highway. It was hypnotically still in the dark. No one ahead of him, no one behind. The gas light blinked on, but Martin figured he could push it. Lisa was snoring softly. She looked good sitting there in the dark. Cheeks smooth. Arms folded neatly across herself. She looked peaceful in a way she hadn't all evening.

Martin took the first bend too fast and the car felt unsteady beneath him. He slowed on the straightaway and was relieved to see another car, its brake lights a friendly face. He followed for several miles. When the tail lights ahead brightened, Martin also applied his brakes. The road stayed straight, but the car ahead continued to slow. Martin pulled into the passing lane, came alongside just long enough to glance over. The driver had his head back. Martin's heart stood still, then the driver, little more than an outline in the dark, turned and looked over at Martin.

Foot down on the accelerator, Martin put distance between himself and that car. He passed a service station, but didn't stop for fear of waking Lisa. By the bridge, the needle stood at empty, but Martin just wanted to get home and into bed. They'd both had a lot to drink. Maybe that's why Lisa was already snoring, and maybe Martin had drunk enough that he shouldn't have been driving.

As he crossed the bridge, Martin looked over at the skyline— a cluster of sky scrapers: bright beautiful buildings cut into the night. Martin drove through the park, rolled down 17th then started climbing the hill. The car spluttered. He gave it gas. He put the pedal all the way down. The engine coughed then stalled. Martin set the emergency brake and tried the ignition. It turned once, twice, then quit. He checked the mirror. Nothing behind him but street lights and parked cars. The car rolled back and he guided it into a spot in front of the church.

Lisa was still asleep.

"Lisa, we're home, Honey." He spoke softly, touched her shoulder, but she didn't move.

Martin walked around to the passenger side and coaxed her out of the car. She groaned something while he kicked the door closed. "Can't you carry me in?" she said then she lifted her head. "Why did you park way down here?"

"Ran out of gas."

"Oh."

She leaned back against the car and rubbed her face. Martin looked up. Here the night sky felt lower, a black tarp tied just above the houses. He drew his arms around himself and also leaned against the car, rested there beside his wife while he gazed up beyond the rooftops.

Pogo started barking before Martin had even unlocked the door. He patted her on the way in, walked through the apartment, and collapsed onto the bed.

Lisa scooped up Pogo and followed Martin into the bedroom. "Your dad was telling me and Carol that these are the best days of our lives."

Martin closed his eyes a moment and realized how sore they were. "I'm tired. Aren't you tired?"

"I was. I'm not now. You think Carol and I will ever become friends?"

"Sure. Of course."

"I'm not so sure."

"You're too sensitive."

Lisa tickled Pogo under the chin. "What do you mean, 'too sensitive'?"

Martin rolled onto his side. "It's three in the morning, Lisa."

Lisa set the dog down and walked to her side of the bed.

"Do you think Scott will give you a job?" she said after a while. "I mean, once you've passed the Bar."

Martin didn't answer. His jaw locked. He swallowed and pretended to be asleep. Eventually Lisa slipped under the covers, and after a time, he took her hand in his, and together they slept.

～

The phone rang just as the sun began to rise. It was Martin's mother. Reflecting on it later, Martin was amazed she was so calm. Among other things, she commented on how thankful she was Carol and Scott had a babysitter that night, how thankful she was the kids hadn't been in the car.

The conversation was short. Martin only asked one question. "Where are they now?" he said, and his mother started to cry short, quiet sobs.

"They took Carol to the hospital. Scott they didn't even try."

"We'll be right up."

Martin was still wearing his shirt and trousers from last night. He couldn't find his shoes and eventually put on sneakers. He was at the door before Lisa had finished dressing.

Last night, the final thing Carol had said to Martin was that the kids had better be asleep by the time they got home. She'd found that funny for some reason. She'd started her donkey laugh. It was a sort of convulsion—Carol with her mouth frozen wide, bent a little as though burdened by her own laughter.

When he reached the car, Martin remembered they didn't have gas. He kicked the door and stood looking at the church. He'd never paid much attention to the place before. It needed a coat of paint. A sign advertised Sunday's services.

Lisa caught up to Martin and pulled on his sleeve. "What about the kids? Who'll take care of Sarah and Johnny?"

Martin put his arms around her, pulled her close and held her. A chill dropped down his spine, and he shivered as he lowered his chin to rest on the crown of her head.

"We have to," Lisa said. "You know it's us that has to."

Even though his mother had mentioned the kids, Martin's mind hadn't touched on them. He'd been thinking of Carol and Scott, their little roadster, of shattered glass, crushed steel, the sight of compacted cars at night. He'd thought of ambulance rides, hospitals, doctors, blood and pain, but until now he hadn't thought of the kids.

Martin's teeth began to chatter. He tightened his arms around Lisa.

In this way, they held each other up, in front of an empty church, beside a car with no gas, at the start of a long journey.

X

A raccoon mauled my mother's cat so badly it cost $300 to stitch him up. The next afternoon, she called to ask if I could help her get rid of the animal. "The vet went on and on about rabies," she said. "What if it bit me? When they get rabies, they go a little batty."

I told her I didn't know how to catch a raccoon. On the sofa across from me, my room mate Alfie raised his arms like he was firing a rifle. "Boom," he said. "Take it out in one shot."

"You rent traps," Mom said. "They come with instructions. All you need is bait."

"When would you want this?"

"Maybe this weekend?"

Her urgency should have told me something more was going on, but at the time I thought nothing of it and said I'd be up Friday evening.

After I hung up, Alfie pushed the bong my way. "Ryan, you can set out traps all month, or take a rifle and be done with it." While I took a hit, he walked into his bedroom, brought back the Lee-Enfield his grandfather had given him. He set it in my hands. "This sucker will blow a raccoon into next week."

I spent a moment getting a feel for the rifle, running my hand down the fine grain of the stock and along the icy barrel, etched and pock-marked by time. Just touching it sent a shiver of electric cold right through my thick dopey haze. Imagine the damage this thing must have done in its lifetime. I raised it to look down the sight line.

"Jesus," Alfie said, "Don't be pointing that at me." He lit the bong, took a hit and batted the smoke away while I laid the rifle across my lap. "Don't even joke about that shit."

Once I was past Orillia, traffic was light. Islands of muddied snow started to appear on the sides of the road. By the time I reached the cottage, the late afternoon sun was sparkling off hardened roadside snow banks that looked like they'd be around for weeks to come.

Mom stepped out to greet me. "You made it," she said as though it had been in doubt. We hugged and she led me up the flagstone path and inside. "You must be tired. All that driving." She squeezed my shoulders then guided me through to the kitchen.

The cottage had been in my father's family for years, but after the divorce it wound up in my mother's hands. Over the past two years she'd rebuilt it, winterized it, modernized it. The doorway where I'd tripped and broken my arm was gone, along with the wall that had divided the kitchen and living area. She'd doubled the size of the deck. The kitchen was all new, including the island, where she was now standing chopping parsley. Her knife built up a steady rhythm. "Now, you must tell me about Sandra," she said.

I tried to read her expression, but her head was down—eyes on her work. "Okay. What do you want to know?"

She looked up, but didn't speak, just lifted a dishtowel and wiped her hands. She seemed to be struggling for words and that put a knot in my throat. Sandy must have told her she was pregnant. Or maybe Sandy's mother had told her. Someone. But all I said was, "I don't really see her much since we broke up," and then I glanced back out the big bay windows towards the lake. It was glassy calm, just the tiniest ripples at its centre.

"Right," Mom said. "Of course."

On the far side of the lake, the last of the day's sunlight reflected off the windows of cottages forming a ragged trail of glinting lights.

"Oh, look at me," she said. Her voice was now high and tight. "I haven't even offered a drink. Wine or beer? I have both."

"Beer." My finger traced a line in the table's dark grain. "Brought a rifle," I said.

"A what?"

"For the raccoons."

"Of course," she said. "The raccoons."

She opened a beer. The cap fell and rolled a few inches along the counter. "Bought the ones you like. With the picture of sail boats." She returned to the fridge and pulled out a bottle of wine.

"Have you been talking to Sandy?" I asked while her back was turned.

"Let me get supper on the table. I shouldn't have started asking about Sandra. I don't know where my mind is." She moved from the fridge to the stove without looking my way. She stirred a pot, tasted something from the fry pan. My mother's thinner than she should be. A wiry woman. She bustles with a frantic energy, especially in the kitchen.

"The reason I ask—" I said.

"—Now hold on a moment, Honey." At the sink, she emptied the pot into a colander. Steam rose in a column and mushroomed above her head. She set the pot aside and turned to face me. She folded her arms, showed her teeth as though forcing a smile. "Truth is last weekend Sandra phoned to invite me to the shower. She thought I knew. At first I didn't understand. I thought maybe this was some strange way of telling me you were back together and getting married. I guess this was just the last thing I expected."

"I'm sorry," I said, although it probably wasn't audible. "I know what you must be thinking. I've been meaning to. Wanting to."

"I'm not thinking anything." She tossed the dishtowel onto the counter. "I'm just glad it's out. I feel relieved." She bowed her head, ran a finger under one eye. "I promised myself I wouldn't cry and now look at me."

My mother stepped forward, set her hands on my shoulders, held me at arms length a moment. A tear formed. I blinked it away, and she pulled me close. Big inevitable tears were on their way, though what I wanted just then, more than anything, was not to be making such a fucking big deal of this. I bit down on my lip, wiped away another tear and told myself to get it together.

"Honey, I know it must be hard, but this is also wonderful news. One day you'll see that." She dug her fingers into my back, held on tight for a moment.

There were a lot of reasons I hadn't told her about the pregnancy. For a time, I wondered if the baby was even mine. Sandy and I were together only once last fall. We bumped into each other at a party. We were drunk. Returning to the apartment we'd once shared was easy and comfortable, though I didn't even stay the night. After she found out, we talked about getting back together, but neither of us really wanted to. I tried to convince her to get an abortion. For the past two months I hadn't seen Sandy at all.

"You don't need to feel ashamed."

"I'm not ashamed. I just. I was planning to tell you this weekend."

"I shouldn't have opened my big mouth. I promised myself I'd give you the weekend to tell me. Or however long you stay. I mean, I was only going to raise the topic when you were leaving." She pulled away. She was trying to smile. "I'd rehearsed being surprised and everything." She threw up her hands and gave me her best surprised look.

The Lee-Enfield is a bolt-action rifle. It fires a .303 cartridge from a five-round detachable clip. 44 ½ inches long, it weighs eight pounds ten ounces unloaded. It has a muzzle velocity of 2,440 feet per second and an effective range of 1,200 yards. It was used by British and Commonwealth forces during both world wars and is still used by the Reserve forces in Canada. The rifle also remains popular with hunters.

∽

After supper, I put a trap at either end of the fence where the raccoons often scrambled. I set a can of tuna in the back of each trap then propped open the door. The moon had ducked behind clouds. On my way to collect the rifle, I tripped over my mother's woodpile.

Holding the Lee-Enfield, hands numb with cold, I practiced raising it, drew a bead on one of my mother's trees and squeezed the trigger. The mechanism clicked. I drew a bead on the half-obscured moon, then lowered the rifle to the streaks of light across the dark water and pulled the trigger again. "Bang," I said.

I left the rifle in the enclosed porch. My mother didn't look up, not as I stashed the bullets in the cabinet, nor as I rubbed my hands together to regain some warmth.

The fire had crumbled into a pile of red coals. Mom was sitting close to it knitting.

"Have you told your sister?" she asked.

I flopped into the armchair and nodded. There was a bowl of cashews on the coffee table. I pulled it closer.

"Oh, Darling, does everyone know but me?"

"I see her every couple of weeks, Mom. It just came out."

"We talk on the phone every week."

"Don't take it personally. There's lots who don't know. I'm going to have to send out a card or something. 'Newsflash: Ryan knocks up ex-girlfriend'."

"Oh, Ryan, for goodness sakes."

The cashews were salted. My favourite.

"What are you knitting?"

"Supposed to be a sweater, but God only knows. It's a disaster. How can a fifty year old learn to knit?" She held it up, a short green flap of material dangled from two needles. "This little kid is just going to melt your heart, Ryan, I swear."

My mother's needles clicked away. I collected cashews in my hand, shook them like dice, popped a couple into my mouth. Just months ago, when I was still pestering Sandy to get an abortion,

I'd said it was the only choice. We were too young. Neither of us wanted to get back together. She finally told me never to talk to her about it again. How do you go from there to having the baby melt your heart?

"You're going to be a great dad," my mother said. "Once you get going."

"I got a letter calculating my child support payments. They start on June 27th. One hundred dollars a week beginning a month after Baby Severin's born."

Her needles stopped. She pulled down her glasses, looked at me above the rims. "The baby won't have your name?"

I shook my head. She pushed her glasses back up and tried to find her place in the knitting. "Maybe you'll get back together."

"She's got a new boyfriend."

This time Mom set her knitting down completely. She looked at me, but no words came out.

"They've moved in together," I said. "The kid will probably be calling him 'Dad'."

"Oh, Ryan, it doesn't have to be that way."

I shrugged. "Not sure I'm wanted."

"Have you given any indication that you want to be involved, like taking an interest in the pregnancy, meeting with the doctors, going to the hospital for the birth? Fathers are now expected in the delivery room. Have you considered that?"

I didn't answer. I mean, what exactly is an unwanted, biological father supposed to do during the birth?

"You know, your father didn't come to Lucy's, but he was there for yours. Times had changed by then and men were allowed in." She took off her glasses, pointed them at me. "It was one of the most important experiences of his life."

"He never told me that."

"Well he told me."

"Alfie bought me a box of cigars."

Mom picked up her knitting. "He's a good kid, Alfie."

I reclined the easy chair and switched on the TV. The cat hopped onto my lap, purring noisily. His thick marmalade fur was shaved where the vet had stitched his wounds. One of his ears was split almost the whole way down.

"I'm going to come," Mom said. "The moment I hear, I'm on my way."

"Great, that way if Sandy wants to scream at someone in the delivery room, you can stand in for me."

"She might not want me in the delivery room, but I'll come as close as I can get."

Raccoons range from 20 to 40 inches long and weigh up to 35 pounds. They are intelligent animals with a well-deserved reputation for mischief—their thumbs enable them to open garbage cans and doors. They carry approximately 50 percent of the documented animal rabies cases in North America. Last year, Toronto police recorded three instances of residents shooting raccoons within city limits.

My alarm sounded at quarter to six. I switched it off and rolled over. When my eyes opened again, the sun was creeping into the sky. I dressed, tiptoed into the hall, loaded the clip and stepped outside. Breath formed clouds in front of my face and my cheeks soon tingled from the cold. I leaned against my car and gazed out towards the road while light spread across the land.

There was no sign of any raccoons and soon the cold had a grip on me. I curled my toes in my boots and shuffled about to keep warm. Once the sun was well over the treeline on the other side of the lake, I laid down the rifle.

At my mother's woodpile, I set a log on the chopping block and picked up her axe. I tested the weight of the axe then swung. The top of the handle hit the wood and sent shock waves back to my hands. On the next swing, I embedded the blade, lifted log and axe wholesale and split it in two strikes.

I chopped wood until I was winded. Blisters were forming on my hands and a warm ache radiated along my arms. The woodpile stood on the high side of the lot and gave a view clear across the lake. Wind formed patterns, broad strokes across the water. Trail-like clouds lay in furrows over the trees. I leaned a hip against the axe and slowly caught my breath, enjoying the chilly breeze on my damp forehead.

I set up another log, swung the axe, split it, and slowly worked myself back into a sweat. Once I was out of breath, I headed for the water. Near the end of the lane, I started to run, pulled off my jacket, sweater and shirt. I arrived at the water stripped to the waist, dropped my pants and pulled off my boots. As I stood on the diving rock, goose bumps rose along my arms and chest, and then, suddenly, I was shivering. When we were kids, before the divorce, we were up here every summer weekend. Our days centred around swimming and eating. Five or six times a day my sister and I dove from this rock. At the time I knew every crack, every sharp corner and smooth edge. All that knowledge was gone, but the rock was still here, below me now, unchanged.

I crouched and dove, hit the water curled almost into a ball. My heart stopped a moment, seized by the cold of the lake; then it began to thunder, knocking against my ribs in quick, heavy blasts. I surfaced with a chest so tight I could only pant. Teeth chattering and body quivering, I managed to turn, paddle in and scramble up the rock. I scraped my knee, stubbed my toe then was out of the water, reborn in the cold morning air.

I tried to pull on my jeans, but it was difficult with wet legs. My fingers were numb and dulled. My entire body shivered in a frigid panic. I wrapped my arms around myself and ran with boots un-laced, collecting my shirt, sweater and jacket on the way up the hill.

The third trimester of pregnancy begins at 28 weeks which is the first week at which a pre-term fetus is considered viable. By 32 weeks, the baby starts to get ready for birth, building fat and turning its head down. At this stage, the baby is about ten inches long and weighs more than a pound. Although its skin is still translucent, the baby's lips, eyebrows, and eyelids are now distinct, and the baby's bones are beginning to harden.

After buying groceries, Mom drove us to a baby store outside Drysdale. We were the only shoppers until a young couple came in. They stood by us while my mother picked out pyjamas. "They're just so tiny," the woman said. "Look how cute."

"Shopping for my first grandchild," Mom said.

The woman looked from my mother to me. I stood there, waiting for the conversation to tumble into humiliating territory—about my age, about not being married, about an unplanned pregnancy. But all she said was, "Congratulations. When's baby due?"

"May 31st."

She put a hand across the top of her belly. "We're May 30th. Isn't that funny?"

The woman's husband pulled her away to look at strollers, and I said, "Why does everything for a baby need a different name? Onesie, sleeper, booties. Why not tee-shirt, pyjamas and shoes?"

"Ryan, don't be such a grump. You sound like your father."

She rifled through another bin of clothes, then lifted a book from a display on the shelf.

"Looks like the one for you," she said. "Get you squared away with your fatherly duties."

That was the first time anyone had even mentioned fatherly duties to me. When I'd asked Sandy what she wanted of me, she'd said, "Nothing. I mean, let's be realistic." Of course, she didn't really mean that, because two months later I got the assessment of child support, which left me facing a Kraft Dinner diet for the next eighteen years. That was the fatherly duty weighing on my mind.

On the way out of the baby store, Mom said, "These clothes are for when you keep the baby. Okay?"

"What's the baby going to do in a two bedroom apartment with Alfie and me?"

"Alfie can help out. It'll be good for him."

"Alfie smokes dope every morning before going to work at a gas station where he sells contraband cigarettes."

"Alfred? Our Alfred?"

"Don't look so surprised."

We climbed into her car and after a few moments of silence, she said, "Perhaps it's time you had your own apartment?"

"Mom," I said.

"One day you'll find someone. Sandy will too, whether it's you or someone else. Raising kids takes all the help available. You need to snap out of it and get involved."

"Alfie marked May 31st on the calendar with a big black X."

"Good."

All the pages before the X used to give me comfort. Now there's just two months left—a thin paper wall slowly vanishing. "It's like that movie about a man who knows he'll have to go to prison on a certain day,"

"This is a baby we're talking about, not a prison sentence."

"I didn't say it was a prison sentence."

"If you're going to be a good father, you need to get up off your duff."

"I'm twenty-four years old."

"I had your sister at twenty-two." She glanced at me quickly. "I don't think I ever told you this, but I was pregnant when we got engaged. And then I miscarried, but we got married anyway and I got pregnant again. The first time I got pregnant, it was like the baby was stealing our youth. Going to be parents at twenty-one. And then when I miscarried, it was like we were robbed again, and so I got pregnant again." She set a hand on my thigh and squeezed. "One day you'll look back on this in a completely different light."

This is how a thirty calibre bullet kills. Travelling at 2,440 feet per second, the energy of the bullet pushes on skin and flesh which stretches until it ruptures enough to allow passage of the bullet. The tissue further dissipates the energy of the bullet by fragmenting and tearing.

While the flesh contracts back to near its original position, the bullet continues to travel through muscle, bone and organs, destroying nearly everything in its path.

Next morning, I was out before the sun was up. And this time I spotted them lumbering beside the fence: a pair of raccoons the size of small dogs. I raised the rifle. My thumb lowered the safety and my finger slipped inside the trigger guard as the sights came in line. I took a bead on the nearest animal, the larger one, and squeezed the trigger. The rifle sounded, kicked against my shoulder and threw me off balance. The nearest raccoon flopped onto its side. It rolled a little. The other dashed under the fence into the shrubs, a waddle sped up so it seemed to lurch from side to side. I slid up the bolt, ejected the spent casing and fired again, but the animal was gone. Walking down the fence line, I fired into the shrub again and again while liquid excitement pumped through my body. Five shots and the clip was empty. My heart began to slow, and I stepped over the dead raccoon. Steam was already rising from a growing pool of blood.

Behind me the cottage door opened and closed. "My God," my mother shouted. "You killed them?" She was still tying a bathrobe around herself.

"Just one."

"You were supposed to trap them not shoot them."

"Mom, this raccoon almost killed your cat."

"That's the mother. You killed the mother."

"How do you know which is the mother?"

She shook her head. "Oh Ryan, I just. Oh God."

"What is it?"

"I don't know. It's sad. They've been my company all winter."

I tucked the rifle's stock under my arm. "What are you doing up here, Mom? With raccoons for company. Raccoons you ask me to get rid of then start crying over."

"I just wanted you to come up." She looked away, raised her

shoulders and shivered. "I wanted to give you a chance to tell your news. It was all I could think of."

"Well, I didn't know. You should have said something."

A woman is considered to be in labour when she begins experiencing strong and regular uterine contractions accompanied by dilation of her cervix. Labour's first stage continues until the cervix is dilated to ten centimetres. The length of the second stage varies from twenty minutes to two hours. During this time, the mother pushes the baby from the womb with contractions spaced three to five minutes apart. This stage ends with the delivery of the baby.

After packing up that afternoon, I kicked the raccoon into a garbage bag. Its body had already stiffened in the cold. I dropped it in the trunk beside the rifle and my overnight bag.

"It's funny to think raccoon skins used to be worth something," Mom said. "The fur."

"Everything used to be worth something."

"Now we just pack it in a garbage bag and drive it to the dump."

"You could skin it and make yourself a hat. Make one for the baby."

"It's just sad how we don't seem to care anymore. No one cares about doing anything. I can't even knit a sweater for my grand-child."

"You've got plenty of time. It's spring. It's going to be summer."

Nodding, Mom stepped closer. She put her arms around me. "Give this grandmother-to-be a big hug, okay. And one for you, wonderful father-to-be." She held me longer than she had in years. I'm not sure which of us broke away, but when we did, she was crying. She wiped each eye. "Oh this is silly."

"I'm going to talk to Sandy about maybe being around for the birth. Or maybe seeing the baby straight afterwards. Guess I should talk to her anyway."

My mother nodded. "Good. That's great. I'm proud of you."

I slid behind the wheel, rolled down my window and waved

and honked as I pulled out of her lane. Once I was on the road, I put on a Moby CD and settled in for the drive.

A stillbirth occurs when a fetus, which has died in the womb or during labour, exits the mother's body. It's still relatively common in Canada, where there are 7.7 stillbirths per thousand. The reasons for most human stillbirths are unknown, but causes include placental abruption, physical trauma, bacterial infection and chromo-somal aberrations.

I got the news the moment I stepped into the apartment. Alfie had already listened to the message and he played it for me. It was Sandy's voice, thin and drawn. "I lost the baby." Her breath echoed through the phone. "And thought you should know."

Alfie had a bong hit lined up on the table. I sat by it, fingered the lighter, while from a great distance, from thousands of miles away, he said, "Dude, you dodged a bad one there."

I tossed the lighter onto the table and leaned back. "I don't know."

One of the tiny outfits Mom had bought was sticking out of the shopping bag, little feet built into the body, snaps all the way down the back. On the front, it said, "Sweet dreams 'til morning."

While Alfie reached for the bong, I pulled out the sleeper. From either side of the sofa, and from a long distance apart, we gazed at it.

MERCEDES BUYER'S GUIDE

When Harry asked, Wayne Krause claimed to know nothing about the stuff in the trunk of the car. He said the car had been his mother's and he hadn't been up to sorting through it after the funeral. He did say that he was pretty sure the microwave worked. When it turned out it didn't, and the toaster wouldn't keep bread down, and both casserole dishes were cracked, Harry suspected that Wayne had piled all that junk in just to get rid of it.

Harry set the kitchenware, the typewriter, the bags of old shoes, the twelve windshield wiper blades and everything else in the corner of his garage. He vacuumed, sprayed air freshener into the car and tried to forget about Wayne Krause. Things kept turning up in that car though, things that kept Wayne and his family at the front of Harry's mind.

The first time Harry adjusted the passenger's seat he found a letter caught in the shifting mechanism. It was dated 12 January 1969. He spent some time wondering how a 1969 letter might have wound up in a 1981 car. Equally strange, the letter complained of heat, drought and dust. It was written as though it was mid-summer. Harry read it to himself three times before taking it inside where he asked Col to guess what he'd just found in the car. Harry knew she didn't want to be disturbed. The kids were asleep and this was her study time, but he asked all the same.

"Another microwave," Colleen said.

Harry shook his head and read it aloud. Along with talk of weather there was mention of Myrna's health, a planned trip to the seaside and a canceled New Years Eve party. "Isn't this neat?"

"Yeah," Colleen said. "Neat."

"I think it's from Australia." Harry re-folded the letter and tapped it against his palm while Colleen marked her spot in one book and turned to read from another. It was still a couple of weeks before exams, but she'd been working like this every night for a month.

"On the radio this morning they said you remember most if you study before sleep," Harry said. "Turns out whatever you were last thinking goes round and round in your brain all night." He waited for a response.

Colleen looked up. She nodded.

"Neat, eh?" Harry said.

Colleen nodded again.

Every night of his life Harry had a shower before bed. Imagine how much smarter he'd be if he'd read the paper or the encyclopedia. Of course, they didn't have an encyclopedia. But still.

A week after finding the letter, while returning the spare tire to its well, Harry found thirty-two hundred dollars in a yellow envelope in the trunk. It was tucked under the lining: hidden, or lost. But that was a week later. Before finding the money, before Harry had even looked at the spare, he took the Australian letter over to Wayne Krause's place. He parked out front and walked across a yard strewn with toys—a trike, wagon, small slide, a couple of hoola hoops. Wayne lived in a cul-de-sac in the Garrison development which meant his kids could leave things lying around like that. It also meant his kids could run around in the front yard without worry. Harry's house was on Bayshore. If Harry's kids left something out after dark it would be gone by morning. And if they stepped off the sidewalk and into the street they'd be dead. A car would zip along and Bang. Harry didn't like to think about it. He didn't appreciate thoughts like this visiting him. It was true though. Zip, bang. Cars traveled way too fast on Bayshore. All the way down green lights fell in line. If Colleen wanted to become an engineer, Harry was fine with that. For starters she could re-engineer the traffic lights on Bayshore.

Harry looked at his watch as he rang the bell. He'd have to make it quick. He hadn't told Col that he was stopping at Wayne's. He counted to ten then rang the bell again. A little girl opened the door, and Harry crouched. "Hi kid, what's your name?"

"Lisa Krause." She was wearing a Barbie tee-shirt.

"That's a sweet name," Harry said. "I'm Harry. Would you tell your Dad that Harry's here?"

"Harry's here," she said, but she was still looking at Harry and she hadn't raised her voice.

"Harry who?" Wayne yelled from somewhere inside.

"Harry Stouffer."

"Stouffer?"

"Like the frozen dinners." That brought no response. "Harry you sold the car to."

That did it. There was movement inside then Wayne appeared, stomping down the hallway: feet, arms and belly all on the move. He looked like a boxer who'd been set loose on the world of dough-nuts and fast food. "I don't know what's wrong with that car, but it was running when I sold it to you—"

"—No, no, it's not about that—"

"—as is, remember. That's what we said."

Harry held up his hands, shook his head and looked down at his feet.

"What?" Wayne said after a pause. "What?"

"You have any family in Australia? Any close family friends or anything?"

Wayne filled the doorframe and the way he was looking at Harry right now made Harry worry about his size. A man that big could really inflict some pain. Harry's scalp warmed.

"Anyone who lived in Australia in 1969?"

Wayne kept looking at Harry in that peculiar way. Harry pulled out the letter. He said it had been under the passenger's seat.

Wayne stepped back into better light, read, flipped the letter over and read the reverse. "Helen," he said.

The salutation was smudged, but the letter had been clearly signed by Helen M. For a moment Wayne stood in silence then he turned.

"Hey, Mer," Wayne yelled. "Get me the phone."

Lisa came out with it. Wayne dialed, stepped into the living room and beckoned for Harry to follow. It occurred to Harry just then that he didn't really want to know who wrote the letter. Not yet. He hadn't spent enough time daydreaming about it; he hadn't even shown it around work. All day it had sat in his glove compartment. And now that it was in Wayne's big fist, Harry was unlikely to get it back.

"Impulse," Harry said out loud. Wayne turned to look at him, but just then someone picked up on the other end and Wayne spoke into the phone. Col often said that Harry had to stop letting impulse carry him away.

Wayne covered the receiver. "Could it be South Africa? It could be, right?"

Harry nodded. Of course it could. That hadn't occurred to him.

"Helen," Wayne said into the phone. "Helen M."

Harry must have assumed Australia because he and Tim had watched a documentary about dingos a couple of months ago, before the TV broke.

Wayne covered the phone again and yelled for someone to get him a map or an atlas or something. Eventually Lisa brought in a map of North America. Wayne un-folded it and turned it over. "Jesus weeps. A world map. A map with frigging Africa on it."

In the end they used a map on the inside cover of a dictionary. Wayne pointed to South Africa as though Harry might not have heard of it. "That's the spot. Right there." His finger covered half the country.

On the verandah Wayne said he was sorry about all the junk in the car. He waved one of his big hands. "I just didn't want to deal with it. My mother's stuff and all. I get emotional about these things." Wayne pinched the bridge of his nose, closed his eyes and gave his head a shake. Harry turned away to give the man some privacy. As he stood gazing down the street, he pictured the collection of wiper blades that still sat in his garage. Who would even have a dozen wiper blades? The rest of the junk Harry sort of understood but a dozen windshield wipers? The screen door banged and Wayne was back inside. He hadn't said goodbye.

When Harry got home, Tim was playing tennis against the wall in the living room and Sashi was bouncing on the sofa singing something from The Lion King. Harry leaned in. "You'll break the springs, Sashi." Thwack. The ball hit the wall only inches from Harry's face. "Cut that out." It rolled under the stereo. Harry headed down the hallway. Thwack. "Jesus weeps." Harry liked that curse. He thought he might start using it regularly.

In the kitchen Colleen had her books out. Thwack. "Jesus weeps," Harry said again.

"What's that?"

"Why don't we just get a new TV? Something cheap."

"It'll rot their minds."

"It'll calm them down. They're tearing the house apart. Just go look at them."

There was a thud that wasn't the tennis ball. Sashi came running into the kitchen and straight into Col's arms. From the living room Tim shouted, "Wasn't me! Wasn't me!" Col rocked Sashi a while then returned one hand to working the calculator. Thwack.

"Tim, do that somewhere else!"

"Where?"

"Outside."

"I'm grounded."

"In the yard."

"It's dark."

The boy thumped down the hallway, poked his head into the kitchen. "What's for supper?"

Oh shit. Harry had forgotten it was his turn to cook tonight. He opened his mouth to suggest they order pizza, but he already knew what Col would say. He turned to the cupboards. "Let me think a sec."

"You didn't stop at the grocery?"

"I thought I'd just make something from what we have here."

Sashi was calm now, but she still leaned into her mother, enjoying the attention. Harry wouldn't have minded some attention. He wouldn't have minded leaning into Col and having her run her hand through his hair. Maybe he should jump up and down and fall off the chesterfield even after someone's told him not to. Thwack.

"Tim, for Christ sakes."

Eggs. He'd make eggs.

Harry diced an onion, grated some cheese, sliced a tomato and set a pan on the stove. He cracked eight eggs, buttered bread then asked Colleen if she could please clear away her books.

When everyone was at the table, Sashi raised her milk. "It's my turn tonight," she announced. "And I want to make a toast to the Queen."

Tim said, "Boring," but it was Sashi's turn so they all raised their glasses.

Harry kept his thoughts about this exercise to himself. With the others he said, "To the Queen."

At ten forty-seven on Saturday 25 April, Harry found thirty-two hundred dollars in the trunk of the car. The day before he'd noticed the rear tires didn't match and he'd wanted to check the spare to see if it was the missing mate. It wasn't, and getting it back into the wheel well proved a bugger. Harry ended up pulling the whole trunk lining off. That's when he noticed the corner of the yellow envelope.

Straight away he knew it was money. And straight away he knew that unless it was Canadian Tire money or something, he had his hands on a good chunk of change. He peeked in. It was full of twenties. His legs went rubbery. He had to sit.

Harry opened one of the lawn chairs, took a load off, and began flipping through the wad. One hundred and sixty twenties ... made thirty-two hundred dollars.

"Jesus weeps."

He'd only paid nineteen hundred. And that was a deal. The car was nearly twenty years old and eaten by rust, but it was still a Mercedes.

Harry tapped the envelope against his thigh with the money tight in his right hand. Thirty-two hundred dollars. Imagine the things you could do with thirty-two hundred dollars. Col would want to put it into savings or a mortgage payment or something. She might be okay spending some on the kids. Horse riding lessons for Sashi. Tennis lessons for Tim. Although Tim didn't really like tennis. He just liked banging the ball against the wall. He liked comic books, but that would be a waste. What about a new television? The boy would love that. Everyone would. It could be a present for the whole family.

Colleen was on the back porch having her one cigarette of the day when Harry stepped out of the garage. At least Harry hoped it was her one cigarette of the day. He didn't want to ask in case she got upset. It was only eleven. It was early to be having her one cigarette. You could bet she'd be needing another by six. She'd be desperate by nine. Harry was considering saying something like that, making it a joke, only then Col turned and noticed him, so instead Harry said, "Guess what I found in the car."

"I don't know. What?"

"Colleen," he said. "Look at me."

Harry threw the money in the air. It took Col a moment to understand what it was, and then she seemed to melt. Harry watched her carefully. More than anything he'd wanted to see Col's reaction. Her eyes grew big and milky. "Harry," she said. "Harry." Her knees went soft, and bent for a moment. Bills fluttered everywhere. It was like hitting big cash in a game show. The air was money.

"Three thousand two hundred dollars," Harry said. Col brought her hands to her mouth. She ran on the spot, jumped up and down, even dropped her cigarette. By now money was blowing all over the muddy yard. They noticed this at the same time. Some bills were already near the fence. Harry chased after them while Colleen bent to gather what was on the porch.

"Kids," she yelled. "Hey kids!"

Harry ran along the fenceline, scooping up bills. When he looked back, Tim and Sashi were standing at the door.

"Help pick up all this money before it blows away!"

For a moment the kids stood watching their parents scramble about then began chasing bills themselves.

When they'd collected all of them, Colleen counted. 158. Two missing. Harry told Tim to hop into Mister Yee's yard, while Sashi crawled under the porch with a flashlight. After Tim found one of the missing bills, they gave up. Harry felt a little bad about losing the other, but when he thought about Col's reaction, it had been worth twenty bucks. She'd melted. She really had.

Inside they had Cokes to celebrate. Colleen proposed a toast. "To thirty-two hundred dollars," she said. They tapped cans and drank.

"To being rich," Tim said.

They tapped cans again and Sashi said, "To being the richest."

After the excitement had died a little, Harry called a family meeting. He'd never called one before. It had always been Col, but today he said they had to decide how to spend the dough.

"Harry," Col said. She touched his shoulder. "Maybe we shouldn't talk about it like this. Maybe we should think about it a while, not do anything impulsive."

"We can discuss it, though," Harry said. "No harm in talking, right? And I wasn't thinking we should spend it all, either. We should definitely put some aside for savings. More than some. A good chunk. Most of it. But I thought we could do something special with the rest. You've been complaining about having to take textbooks out of the library, so why not buy some? Sashi's been wanting riding lessons and Tim—"

"—A TV," Tim said. He said it right on cue. It couldn't have been better if they'd planned it. Harry clapped his son on the back. "That's an idea." He couldn't remember when he'd been happier with something Tim had said. "A TV," the boy said again. It gave Harry a pinch of regret for having grounded him. He'd overreacted. He saw that now. The lamp had been old—worthless really.

"Maybe that could be the present to the whole family. The rest goes to savings or to the mortgage." Harry was trying to make it seem like he hadn't thought this through.

"Harry." Col wasn't buying. She shook her head, but then Tim started chanting: "TV, TV." When Sashi joined in, Harry couldn't help but grin.

"Some text books too," Harry said, pointing at his wife.

"Everyone," Col raised her voice, but Tim and Sashi kept chanting and banging on the table. Harry took the money out and threw it in the air. It filled the room, rose to the lamp, and fluttered ground-ward like dead leaves. Tim stood to bat at the bills. Sashi began running around the kitchen. Finally Colleen broke into a smile and started nodding. She scooped up some money, threw it in the air, scooped up more, and threw it at Harry.

By four thirty-six that afternoon, they were all watching the new television. *Lassie* was on. Without cable there weren't many options. Harry couldn't find his glasses, but the screen was big enough that he could do without. He was just thinking how he'd want them for the hockey tonight when it occurred to him that there might be more money in the car. Think of all the things they'd left in there:

a microwave, a toaster, typewriter, shoes, an old letter and a wad of cash. Obviously not very careful people. Obviously not very well organized. Not that Harry was either of these things, and not that he was complaining, but still.

"What if there's more money in there?" Harry said during the next commercial. "What if they were really rich and just had lots of cash lying here there and everywhere? They had a Mercedes after all. Plus at least thirty-two hundred in cash."

"We have a Mercedes and thirty-two hundred in cash," Tim said.

Harry patted him on the knee. "You're right there, son." And then Harry stood. "Who wants to help me search the car?" No one answered. Harry said, "Who wants more money?" and Tim's ears perked up. "If I find more money, who do you think should keep it?"

Tim stood. "Whoever wants some money had better come help." Good old Tim. It was nice to be getting along so well. They'd had a lot of fights recently, and that whole incident with Grandmother's lamp still hung over them.

In the end they all went. Colleen put on rubber gloves and groped between the seats. She found some tissue, a pen, a pair of broken sunglasses and an unsigned birthday card for a ninety-five year old.

Tim searched the doors—their pockets, handles, trim panels, armrests and ashtrays. Harry gave Sashi the flashlight and coerced her into searching the trunk. He told everyone to keep an eye out for his glasses, then began removing the front seats. He knew this was taking things a bit far, but he wanted to be thorough. By the time he had the second one out, Col and Sashi had gone back inside. Tim was just watching. There was nothing of interest under either seat. Tim tried sitting in one. The springs gave an old man's sigh.

Harry crouched where the passenger seat had been and emptied the glove compartment. Stuck in a crevice was a driver's licence for Barbara Krause. In the picture she looked startled and pale. It had expired in 1988. Harry held it up to show Tim, but his son had left too.

Harry removed the dashboard cover and poked about the instrument panel's wiring, the heater unit, the passages that led to the vents. He began on the steering column then realized it was seven o'clock. It was also a Saturday which meant it was his turn to cook. He walked in whispering, "Pizza, pizza, pizza." Tim and Sashi screamed their approval but minutes later bickered over the toppings as they always did.

It was while tipping the deliveryman that Harry realized the money hadn't been lost or misplaced. No one would misplace thirty-two hundred dollars. They'd hid it deliberately. Old people always hid money. They distrusted banks. And if the Krauses had hidden more, wouldn't it be somewhere unusual? He'd have to search the entire car. Every inch.

Harry didn't watch Hockey Night in Canada. Instead he removed the roof paneling, pulled up the carpeting and took the trim off the doors. He checked the rusty bumpers, the rusty wheel wells, looked over the whole rusty underbody. He removed one piece of the side molding just to assure himself nothing could fit in it. He didn't give up until five past eleven by which time half the car seemed to be strewn about the garage. Harry hadn't found a penny. He hadn't even found his glasses.

～

On 16 September 1980, a silver Mercedes 126-S rolled off the S-Class line at the Daimler-Benz plant in Sindelfingen, West Germany. It was near the end of the second shift. The red light had been on all day indicating the assembly line was behind quota. What was more, it was Torsten Fast's birthday and his family would soon be gathered and waiting for him. All the same, Torsten took his time on this last car, examined its heating and air conditioning systems, its instrument cluster and steering column then noticed a piece of paper lying on the floor. He bent and lifted it. "*Glückwünsche zu Deinem Geburtstag!*" Torsten looked about, smiled self-consciously, tucked the note into his pocket and turned fully around. No one was watching. He patted the car and moved on.

Torsten gave every car he inspected a tap on the hood. He called it his *letzter Kuss*.

The car left the plant by train, bound for the port of Bremer-haven, and traveled to Montreal by container ship where it cleared customs and was inspected, tagged and transferred to an eighteen-wheeler at the Mercedes preparation centre. While driving it onto the trailer, Martin Roche brushed it against a concrete pillar. He'd been adjusting the radio so he could listen to something for the few seconds it took to move the car. The contact left a small scrape and a shallow dent, but Roche was the only person to notice. His palms grew damp and his stomach did somersaults until after the driver had signed for the cars and was headed for Markham. The moment the truck was out of the prep centre that scrape could have happened anywhere. Roche swore up and down that he'd be more careful. He'd only had the job two weeks and at this rate he wouldn't last long.

The silver 126-S arrived along with two C-class sedans and a station wagon at the Frank Cherry dealership next morning and Frank had a fit. He spotted the scrape straight off. He had an eye for that sort of thing. He said he'd send it back, said he'd send the whole load right back to fucking Germany. His son-in-law told him they could fix it, but Frank wasn't listening. He gripped his chest. Was someone trying to kill him? Didn't they know he had a heart condition? Frank was at the loading entrance, but customers could still hear. Barbara Krause blushed. The man had to be seventy and here he was carrying on like a ten-year-old. She tried not to listen. On the way back into the show room Frank Cherry said he wanted someone fired for this. His face was bright red. Cherry, Barbara thought.

∾

Tuesday evening Harry remembered to stop at the grocery store. He picked up sausages, potatoes and a head of cabbage. The Garrison development was only a couple K away and Harry found himself turning towards Wayne's place. All the toys were still out on the lawn. It had been a week, but they seemed to be in exactly the same spots.

Lisa answered the door. Harry crouched. "Would you tell your dad that Harry's here?"

"Harry who?" Wayne called.

"Stouffer. Like the frozen dinners."

Wayne stepped into the hall. He wiped his mouth with a serviette.

"I'm sorry," Harry said. "Hope I'm not interrupting anything. Not eating are you?"

"No, no, come on in. Find any more letters?" Wayne chuckled. "My sister and I got a real kick out of that." The screen door banged behind Harry.

"I was just driving by and thought I'd. I just wanted to know. I could have called for this, but I lost your number. Hi, Lisa." Harry was having trouble getting to his question. He was no longer even sure what it was. He wanted to know something—about the elderly parents who'd hidden money in their car, the great aunt living in South Africa, the startled face staring out of the driver's licence, the birthday card for a ninety-five year old and the windshield wiper blades.

Wayne was still staring at Harry. Lisa was staring at him. Neither seemed to blink. Harry dug both hands into his jacket pockets, then he felt the taped arm of his second pair of specs. He shifted from foot to foot trying to figure out how to ask, where to start.

"Harry?" Wayne said, and Harry took a deep breath. "Something wrong, Harry?"

"I can't find my glasses. I didn't leave my glasses here did I?"

"He leave his glasses here?" Wayne called over his shoulder.

"No."

Harry nodded. He nodded as hard as he could and said he wouldn't bother them again. He waved to Lisa and waited for her to wave back. She didn't.

~

Ken Krause liked the idea of a scraped car. He liked the idea of saving a grand for a scrape and a dent which they could fix and make imperceptible. Plus there'd be no waiting list. It could be his today. Barbara wasn't so sure. Wouldn't it decrease the resale value? Wouldn't it rust? And didn't it seem strange to spend thirty thousand dollars on a damaged car? She didn't say all of this, at least not in so few words. She said she didn't like silver. Too flashy, too much glitter. And she spent a long time standing near the one she did like. It was deep green and in perfect condition. Eventually she pulled Ken aside and asked if they shouldn't at least look at some others.

"Lovey, I'm negotiating. Just let me take care of this. Please." But Barbara could see that the only thing Ken was taking care of was that silver car. They'd be stuck with it. She knew it.

In the lounge, Barbara lit a cigarette. She shouldn't be upset. It was a brand new car except for the scrape. But it bothered her all the same. For one thing, Jeannie would notice no matter how they painted it. Remember last year when she spotted that mark on Eloise's gown? It was tiny and they'd all but removed it, but in the end Eloise was in tears and blaming Barbara for spilling the mascara and ruining her wedding.

When Barbara returned to the showroom, Ken had the silver car on the street ready for a test drive. The two of them circled the nearby blocks then drove the highway a mile in each direction. Ken said it was an Arabian thoroughbred on wheels. Barbara said as little as possible. They parked in the lot. Ken went in for the paperwork. He asked if she wanted to join him. Barbara shook her head and lit a cigarette. She switched on the radio. Ken was almost an hour in there, and when he came out he had a toothy, owner's grin. He raised the keys, suddenly a little boy holding the best present ever. It lit her heart a moment. He offered the keys. "Do the honours?" But Barbara shook her head.

Ken pulled out of the lot and made a right onto Hossler Road. Barbara put a hand on his leg, let it lie there. She wanted to ask when they were going to fix the dent, but held back. Two blocks from the highway a snowball hit the windshield. A second hit the hood with a deep thud. Ken slammed the brakes, brought the car to an abrupt halt. Barbara wasn't wearing her seat belt. Her body hit the dash. Her face hit the windscreen. Straining against his own belt, Ken lost his breath. His heart sputtered, clamoured against his rib cage. When the momentum was spent, Ken fell back against the seat and Barbara fell from the dash. She lifted a hand, groped at the arm rest and pulled herself up.

"You all right?" Ken said in a whisper.

"Yes. I think." She didn't say anything else. She ran fingers across her body, brought them to her face and sat slumped in the passenger seat.

"Goddamn kids. Jesus."

Ken unbuckled and climbed out of the car. He brought a hand to his chest. That had scared him. It really had. His knees were trembling. All through his body he could feel it. Jesus, what a scare.

No one in sight. That was always the way. As soon as he drove off, the little fuckers would be back. A car passed, horn blaring. Ken got back in, and pulled over to the curb. Barbara lit a cigarette.

"Give me one of those, will you?" Ken said.

Barbara nodded, passed him hers and lit another.

"Jesus." Ken banged a hand against the steering wheel and that too hurt.

∾

When Harry got home that night, the TV was on. Tim and Sashi were quiet in front of it, their faces illuminated by the flashing screen. Down the hall, Col was studying at the kitchen table. Harry set the grocery bag on the counter and said he was making bangers and mash. He put a pot on the stove, peeled the potatoes, cut them in half so they'd cook more quickly then sliced the cabbage and tossed it in the frying pan with the sausage.

Barbara Krause's driver's licence lay on the counter. Harry lifted it as the kids came down the hall for supper. For a moment, the sound of Col laying out the cutlery evaporated and in that moment Harry glimpsed beyond Barbara's startled face and into a sorrow that lay beneath it. For an instant it could have been his own face in that licence, his wife's, even one of his kids'. It made Harry want to go back into the garage and sift through all those things which had cluttered the car, look for something he might have missed, not money, something more personal, something that would testify for Barbara: further evidence she'd been here, engaged and participating.

Col and the kids were seated and waiting. When Harry turned, he saw them, and set down the licence, walked to the table and raised his glass. "To Barbara Krause," he said. "Whoever she was."

For a moment, his children and his wife just gawked. In all the weeks they'd been making toasts, Harry had never offered one, but now he held steady with his glass in the air until one by one the family raised their cups and toasted Barbara Krause. They drank their milk and finally, Harry sat.

ESPLANADE
Books

THE FICTION SERIES AT VÉHICULE PRESS

[Andrew Steinmetz, editor]

A House by the Sea : A novel by Sikeena Karmali

A Short Journey by Car : Stories by Liam Durcan

Seventeen Tomatoes : *Tales from Kashmir* : Stories by Jaspreet Singh

Garbage Head : A novel by Christopher Willard

The Rent Collector : A novel by B. Glen Rotchin

Dead Man's Float : A novel by Nicholas Maes

Optique : Stories by Clayton Bailey

Out of Cleveland : Stories by Lolette Kuby

Pardon Our Monsters : Stories by Andrew Hood

Chef : A novel by Jaspreet Singh

Orfeo : A novel by Hans-Jürgen Greif
[Translated by Fred A. Reed]

Anna's Shadow : A novel by David Manicom

Sundre : A novel by Christopher Willard

Animals : A novel by Don LePan

Writing Personals : A novel by Lolette Kuby

Niko : A novel by Dimitri Nasrallah

Stopping for Strangers : Stories by Daniel Griffin

Véhicule Press
www.vehiculepress.com